THE TEARDOWN

The Teardown

A NOVEL

David Homel

ESPLANADE BOOKS

THE FICTION IMPRINT AT VÉHICULE PRESS

ESPLANADE BOOKS IS THE FICTION IMPRINT AT VÉHICULE PRESS

Published with the generous assistance of the Canada Council for the Arts, the Canada Book Fund of the Department of Canadian Heritage, and the Société de développement des entreprises culturelles du Québec (SODEC).

SODEC
Québec

Canadä

Canada Council   Conseil des arts
for the Arts   du Canada

The author would like to thank the Conseil général du Nord, France, for the residency it offered at the Villa Marguerite Yourcenar.

This novel is a work of fiction. Any resemblance to people or events is coincidental and unintended by the author.

Esplanade Books editor: Dimitri Nasrallah
Cover design: David Drummond
Typeset in Minion and Filosofia
Printed by Marquis Printing Inc.

LIBRARY AND ARCHIVES CANADA CATALOGUING IN PUBLICATION

Homel, David, author
The teardown : a novel / David Homel.

Issued in print and electronic formats.
ISBN 978-1-55065-520-9 (softcover).– ISBN 978-1-55065-526-1 (EPUB)

I. Title.

PS8565.O6505T43 2019   C813'.54   C2018-906749-7
C2018-906750-0

Published by Véhicule Press, Montréal, Québec, Canada

Distribution by LitDistCo
www.litdistco.ca

Printed in Canada on FSC® certified paper.

*Give Chicago half a chance, and it will turn
you into a philosopher.*

–Saul Bellow in 1983, upon discovering his
childhood home was now a lot full of rubble

ONE

PHIL BRENNER RAPPED SOFTLY at his daughter's door. He hoped he had been soft about it, though it sounded deafening. He wanted to tell Dana he was going out for the evening, though normally she would have no use for that information. She lived independently under his roof, he and his wife's, after spending a brilliant year at university and then dropping out.

"Access denied," he heard her call.

He opened the door and went in. Dana was lying on her bed, fully dressed, shoes on. They were urban hiking boots, the soles clean from underuse. She had a sheaf of papers next to her, and more were on her desk, the same wooden model she had had since girlhood.

"May I?" he asked.

It was a game between them, though Phil had not yet figured out the exact point of it.

He picked up a sheet of paper from the bed. It was the last page of an academic article printed off the net. The page contained the conclusions and the beginning of the bibliography. He was curious. He was a journalist, though he hadn't worked much lately. His specialty was the prestigious long form, the "think piece," and he had experience with this kind of research. He investigated hard cases, though lately there was less demand.

Cryptomnesia, he read. *Family romance.*

It was not easy to tell what was going on in the article from the last page. Academics were not great writers, and this one ended his essay with all the grace of a car crash. Though from the page he held, he learned that Freud had not invented the term "neurosis" after all. Society owed that to someone Phil had never heard of, a certain William Cullen who coined it in 1769, more than a hundred years before the Viennese doctor burst on the scene. The author of the article had little use for neurosis and its sufferers, who included just about everybody, and maybe that was the problem with it. He called it "a rag-bag of symptoms and 'functional' conditions." Phil smiled at the word "rag-bag." It did not sound very professorial.

He read on and hit this sentence just before the end: "The self-traumatized perpetrator—victim and patient—is no longer tenable, only hateful."

"Where did you get this?" he asked his daughter.

"Online."

"You mind if I look at the first page?"

His daughter handed it to him, and he sat at the matching wooden chair in front of her desk, her girlhood furniture. The author was an anthropology professor, not a mental health professional, a certain Allan Young from McGill University in Montreal. "The Self-Traumatized Perpetrator" was the article's title.

"I don't get it," he said to Dana.

"You know how the Internet is, or you should know. I find references to my field everywhere."

"You could have stayed in university. You could have lived in this world with all its comforts."

It was a useless thing to say, and he knew it, since he had said it before, to no effect. His daughter had enrolled in the history department of a top university, and enjoyed an extraordinary first year. Phil was happy, here was a family resemblance, she might just follow his path. Then, in her History of the Soviet Union survey class in second year, when the time came to move on and leave the Ukrainian famine of the early 1930s for the next disaster, the Second World War, she refused to follow the class. She had been producing chronicles of the famine ever since, and for that work she found she did not need the classroom.

Her professor was a kindly man, and troubled by his student and her illogical decision. He wrote Phil and his wife Amy a note expressing his sadness. Here was a talented young woman with great potential who was seemingly crippled by an obsession, and university procedures made it impossible for him to give her anything but a failing mark. He had urged Dana to register with the Handicap Office, he told her parents. The Office might find a way to accommodate the girl. But Dana was not interested in being accommodated.

The concerned professor used the word "obsession" in the usual popular way, a little sloppy for an intellectual. Dana did not have an obsession. She had something else. Phil was not sure what. But he was convinced that his daughter could not be the perpetrator of anything. She did not go out of the house often enough. But self-traumatized, yes, that was how she seemed to him.

When Dana showed no interest in writing anything but her own famine histories, the professor came up with a logical idea. Though he would regret losing her, Dana Brenner could switch over to the creative writing program within the English Department. It was a way of keeping her in university, and he would put in a good word for her, he played tennis with the

11

chairman of English who would probably give her credit for the work she had done in his department.

Phil mentioned the offer. He had not seen her so angry since she'd been a child.

"Creative writing—that's fiction. It's an insult. This isn't fiction. It's real."

She was in such a righteous rage that Phil did not dare tell her a woman had won the Nobel Prize for doing just the sort of thing she was doing. Her name was Svetlana Alexievich. Dana must have come across her online.

He handed her back Page One of Mr. Young's family romance.

"I'd have to read the whole text, and even then," he said carefully. "I can't imagine what this is about."

When his daughter puzzled him, and that happened more frequently lately, it was better to retreat and claim lack of knowledge than make a wrong guess about the particular construction she was devising.

"The Self-Traumatized Perpetrator," she cited. "It means what it says. Somebody who commits a crime, and is traumatized by his own violence."

"'No longer tenable, only hateful.'"

"I noted that. Whoever the guy is who wrote this is a real moralizer."

He wondered what use this piece was to his daughter, but that investigation would have to wait.

"I'm going out now. My group is having a little party."

"Your group. Of course. Well, don't fall."

He stopped. His hand fell away from the doorknob.

"What's that supposed to mean?"

"You're leaving a safe place and going out into the world. There are dangers."

He took a step back to the bed where she lay, surrounded by papers. He drew a printed sheet off her bedspread.

"People are getting traumatized by their own crimes. There are dangers here too."

"I can manage them. Outside, that's impossible. Someone could brush up against me in the crowd."

"That's exactly the kind of thing I enjoy."

She looked at him incredulously. Her father's male enjoyment was not her affair. "Don't fall."

"Too late, I've already fallen."

"That's what you think."

He left his older daughter and went down the hall. His wife Amy was in the bedroom. He heard voices on the TV, a man and a woman locked in domestic drama. They were hissing at each other, the woman's voice dominant, or so it sounded to him. His relationship would not make much of a series. *Scenes from a Marriage*, maybe—he and Amy would need a director on par with Bergman to draw out the drama from their everyday subtleties. He called out that he was leaving, and she acknowledged that from behind the door.

The self-traumatized perpetrators were not the best send-off for an evening Phil Brenner was not sure he wanted to be part of. He had sworn he would not attend his grief counsellor's soirée. A group of strangers bound together by loss, or their sense of loss, more to the point, assembled for a drink on an early Friday evening. And not at a bar with an indulgent bartender, but in the therapeutic confines of Dr. Anne Sheridan's living room where all emotions would be subject to rigorous interpretation.

Whenever he spoke to Dr. Sheridan, and that was more often these days, that feminist invention from the 1960s came to mind: *therapist = the rapist*. That was a piece of graffiti spray-painted on the white limestone wall of the Social Sciences Pavilion at his university, presumably because the building housed the Psych Department that churned out male members of the helping professions who would go out into the world and use the power vested in their diplomas to oppress women.

Now the therapist was a woman. Women had taken back therapy since the days of that graffiti. They were joining fast-acting therapeutic groups led by people like Dr. Sheridan when they weren't creating their own ones. It was a revolution in self-care. Something had changed, maybe thanks to the writers of that graffiti.

"An evening with the bereaved," Phil had said when she'd issued the invitation. "How could I resist?"

"We do the work of grief ourselves, each of us, that much is true," Dr. Sheridan allowed. "But resilience, which is so important to us, is the product of community. That much has been shown over and over again."

Phil glanced at the clock on her table, oriented toward her, but still visible to him. She could have made the invitation once their fifty-minute hour was up, in that narrow window between appointments, instead of using his time. He had an old-country sense of economy, the inheritance from his parents' parents, and it proved useful in the freelancer's life. How does she do it? he thought, moving from one member of the loss community to the next, keeping all the details straight. Or were everyone's stories the same?

"As well," she pushed on, "we all believe our loss is like no one else's. But loss is universal. It defines us as human beings. That's why I think it's worthwhile for my patients to come together and meet in an informal setting. Summer will be here soon, and people will be off on their own."

Phil Brenner hated being referred to as a patient. Patients were ill people, and he had no illness. His daughter's ever-changing disorders had brought him here, and with them, the feeling that she was lost to him. He consulted Anne Sheridan only when necessary, when he hit a particularly thorny sticking point in his relationship with Dana—when their exchange became intolerably one-sided, when his oldest daughter retreated into a place where he could not follow her, when he grieved for her, like tonight, with her self-traumatized perpetrators, whoever they were. His sessions were scattered, and scheduled as needed. Anne Sheridan was flexible when it came to her favourite patients, the ones willing to accept her theory, which held that loss defines what it means to be human. Phil could agree with that. He had seen as much in his work. And the definition was so wide it allowed just about everyone on two legs to be her patient.

"You are exhibiting resistance," she told him.

"That sounds like a painting on a wall. A work of art." He attempted to mime an abstract sculpture at an exhibition.

Anne Sheridan smiled thinly. Freud, Lacan, the old masters of analysis she considered outmoded, loved word play. To her it was just a way of avoiding the real issues.

"Okay, okay, I'll show up. How do I dress?"

"A man does not have to ask that question. As always, come as you are."

Phil wanted Dr. Sheridan to like him. There was an inner circle of chosen ones, and he wanted to be part of them. He knew that drive, knew it was called transference, and accepted its hold on him. What was wrong with wanting to be liked by someone you admired?

But one enduring conflict remained between them, and so far it had no resolution. Anne Sheridan wanted Phil to bring

15

his wife to a session. And Amy would not surrender her claim that she needed no help with loss.

No, that was not what she said. That was Dr. Sheridan's interpretation. Amy believed she had no loss. The trouble was with her daughter, her daughter's mind and body. Therefore, logically, Amy did not need that kind of group that gave off the stink of New Age.

The time he spent sitting in the quiet of Anne Sheridan's basement office, the hum of the dehumidifier adding the white noise that covered their conversation, that was precious to Phil. So was his wife. He was a man of divided loyalties. Sometimes he saw his wife's claim through his therapist's eyes, and holding a critical view of the woman he'd once idealized, and sworn fidelity to, troubled him. Other times, marriage clearly gave Amy the upper hand. In the night, at dawn, whenever he could, for years he would reach for Amy's body, not Anne Sheridan's. Yet he believed in the idea of loss and its usefulness. It was an approach to life, it brought order and self-understanding. It was more than a psychologist's slogan.

But he would not push the members of his family to share his conviction. He dug in against Dr. Sheridan and would not urge Amy to come with him. And he wouldn't allow her to enrol his younger daughter Megan either, though he realized that Dana's disorder could be considered a loss for her sister.

"I am not going to make my counselling a family affair," he declared.

Anne Sheridan said nothing. She didn't need to. She and Phil listened to his words hanging in the air, refusing to settle, floating there with all their understandable falseness.

But now, on this evening, he was happy to be with the grief group, out of his house with its perils and into Dr. Sheridan's, mingling his loss with other people's. The décor at her place was convivial and cultured, an effortless sense of ease with the right art magazines displayed on the cabinets, periodicals that Phil had never written for. He stepped up to the wine table. A meagre, entry-level confrerie of Rioja bottles, red and white, stood surrounded by a wall of domestic mineral water. Most of the guests were concentrated there, homing in on the wine, filling their plastic goblets. There was little taste among the partygoers for the sparkling water, except for those whose loss had gotten tangled up with and magnified by alcohol.

Phil had studied the phenomena, and he did not have to make the calculation anymore. There were always more takers for white than red. White was more refreshing, it was an early-evening drink, an aperitif. It did not stain the teeth or leave a smudge on the mouth like lipstick after a kiss. He reached for the red.

He quickly drained the first glass, and without looking to see if any fellow partygoers were watching as he filled another one. He held it casually, sniffing its bouquet in mock sophistication, pretending it was his first, and only a prop. He waited. He did not have to wait long. The tension slipped from his shoulders. His movements felt more fluid. A buzz of molecules formed a transparent curtain between him and the room like snow on an old-time television set. The first drink was in him. The evening could begin.

He often wondered if this was a danger sign, the anticipation and pleasure he found in the first glass. No, he decided. It was not. It was simply a way of doing business with the world. What was the designation? *High-functioning.* I am a high-functioning person. Not like the college teacher he knew who took a bottle to bed with him that, amazingly, his wife tolerated. When liver malfunction caused his body cavity to fill with blood that turned black in the no-man's land between his internal organs, Phil was the only one who would drive him to the hospital with the promise of a drink on the way, set up on the open glove compartment door. Now that was non-functioning. That was loss of self. He was not that kind of person.

In the midst of that meditation a woman stepped between him and the wine table, and disproved all his observations about the behaviour of attendees at receptions. She poured herself a glass of red, then another, and displayed no vanity when it came to wine stains.

Phil looked at her hands.

"You're a two-fisted drinker," he said to her.

"I'm drinking for two."

"You're pregnant?" he marvelled. She had to be ten or fifteen years past child-bearing age.

"Right—with God's seed!"

"If you feel bad, don't do things that will make you feel worse."

"You can actually recite Anne's mantras. Amazing."

The woman broke a smile. She clearly did not think it was unseemly to mock her therapist's favourite lines under her own roof, and with Anne close by, maybe within earshot. He was a little envious. Wanting to be liked by Anne Sheridan kept him solidly in check.

"This glass is for my imaginary friend," the woman said.

She took a quick sip from it. The wine stained her teeth purple, and she made no move to wipe away the colour.

"So, what did you lose?" she asked. "The best way to start the evening is with our loss. You go first."

Phil could not answer. He was still back with the self-traumatizing perpetrators. He could not bear to say his daughter's name, nor that it was his daughter, and what the issue might be.

"I know: you've lost me," the woman said.

She turned her back on him and walked into the centre of the room, the wine threatening to brim over onto her two small fists.

He watched her move away, slipping past the glass-covered coffee table. A black pleated skirt, tan-coloured tights, a pastel sweater. Mohair, he thought. He didn't know mohair still existed.

He saw the woman creating community across the room with a large, bulky, rumpled man who stood out in this crowd of slim, well-maintained men, and women fighting the good fight of self-image. He looked like a truck driver who spent too much time sitting down, or an ex-football player. What had that guy lost, his knee ligaments?

By the time he circled back to the wine station, all the white was gone. The partygoers were settling for red, despite its stain danger and the sour way it rode the breath. The last bottle surrendered no more than a half-glass, which was maybe just as well for driving. When he looked up, Anne Sheridan was observing him. He raised his plastic goblet in her direction. She did not return the toast. One step and she was at his side.

"I have thought about your idea and, really, it would not be appropriate. And I think you know that. You are free to write about yourself and your process. Your family's process. I can imagine that would be of interest to people, and to yourself too, of course. But not about this group, the people here tonight."

"I don't do that kind of self-journalism. I do political."

"Yes, I know. I have read your prize-winning pieces. You come across as fearless."

Phil looked away from Dr. Sheridan. He was one of those people who could take an insult, but not a compliment.

"I didn't know you read my stuff."

Anne Sheridan smiled. "Everything's online. There's Rate-My-Shrink, and every other possible survey. We can check up on our patients too. It's only fair."

"I suppose so. Fearless, no. But in some circumstances you lose all sense of danger. Your work makes you feel invincible. It's crazy to think that way, of course."

"Crazy?" Dr. Sheridan wasn't fond of the word. "It's a symptom of post-traumatic stress disorder."

"I don't have it anymore," Phil defended himself. "I've stopped throwing myself into risky situations."

Despite the fascination of the topic, Dr. Sheridan's attention was wandering, the signal, most likely, that their conversation was over. Perhaps each patient—Phil hated the label but there was no other way to name what he was to her—had a set allotment of time. Sheridan, he saw, was observing the woman with the two wine glasses and the rumpled, bulky man. He envied what the therapist knew. She had the story he was chasing.

"Who is she?"

"Lynne."

"I see."

"You're not going to ask his name?"

"I haven't talked to him yet."

The next minute Lynne came over to them. "My antennae are buzzing like crazy. Am I missing something?"

"This gentleman asked me for your name."

"Lynne." She held out her hand to Phil.

Dr. Sheridan stepped away from them smoothly and wished them a pleasant evening.

"You're right," Phil told Lynne, "I did lose you. But now you've come back."

She leaned near him, close to his shoulder, as if to demonstrate. "White pepper. You smell like white pepper. That's amazing. What man has ever smelled like that?"

She spoke in a stage whisper. Phil was not the only one who heard, and that was the point. Lynne's grief could be instantaneously converted into desire; it was a process close to alchemy. If love could pitch its tent in the place of excrement, then loss could be eroticized. Finally, something was happening to jazz up this static event.

"If my loss was you, what was your loss?" he asked.

"Is. What *is* my loss? You should know that by now. It's always in the present." She put her hand on Phil's arm. "But tell you what. I don't want to talk about it right now. For once, let's not play show and tell."

Phil was just as happy to take the night off. Whatever it was that had happened to Lynne, it could hover in the air around her, around both of them, like a cloud of musk, like patchouli. He still loved patchouli, that oily perfume that accompanied the loves of his younger years. Just this week in a shopping mall, he had walked behind a girl wearing it, and his mouth watered. He could imagine how eroticizing loss worked after all. He had just done it.

Whatever had happened to Lynne... Dr. Sheridan would not have approved of the formulation. If loss is what makes us human, then it does not happen to people, to Lynne or himself, any more than being born happens to people. Loss was simply the price of the ticket of admission. But somewhere, in some part of his psyche he tried to keep hidden from Sheridan, Phil still believed that loss fell upon a person like a tree limb, a slap in the face, a rebuke from fate for some misstep, past or present.

Lynne gazed at the Rioja bottles, all exhausted, red and white both.

"She's not much of a provider."

"I guess that's the point. Not to get too comfortable."

There was probably a paragraph in the grief counsellor's manual that set down the proper level of intoxicating beverages to be served at a reception. Just enough to create the want for more, but no more than that. Let the thirsty go elsewhere if they must—preferably back to their hearths. The etiquette of inviting patients into the home must be delicate. What happened if they did not want to leave, if they acted out, if their super-egos failed and they made for the spare bedroom when the hostess had her back turned? Was there a Mr. Sheridan, and if so, had he been sent out to spend the evening at a sports bar? Or was he among the losses, which might explain the branch of counselling Dr. Sheridan had chosen. At each session, Phil asked after her health and general disposition, which he considered basic politeness, but she clearly judged it as prying, a sinister form of transference. She never answered, not even with a pat, polite formula, and steered the subject back to him.

He picked up a bottle of red that had been shunted toward the back of the table. By its weight, he understood it was not fully empty.

"We're in luck." It made a respectable serving in Lynne's glass. "But our fearless leader doesn't want us to settle in for the night."

"Then we ought to go somewhere else where we're more appreciated."

"Okay, but just one. I'm driving. I have to stay on the right side of sobriety."

"Best of luck," she wished him.

"No table service," the barmaid shouted at them as they walked into the bar in the strip mall. "Waitress went home."

The bar attempted a Roaring Twenties motif, with posters declaring the arrival of Prohibition followed by its repeal, and a scattering of mass-produced Al Capone memorabilia. The poster advertising the film about the Saint Valentine's Day Massacre appeared at several spots on the wall. The place was inexplicably called the Doll's House. Ibsen's contained domestic drama—or maybe it was Katherine Mansfield's—meets the American romance of violence.

It was anybody's guess why the owner of the Doll's House had gone for the Prohibition motif. The décor had no relation with the exurban world outside its doors. The customers, Phil and Lynne included, lived in tracts designed by developers who must have suffered from claustrophobia, and needed vast planes of space to stem their anxieties. Houses had devoured the farmland, a few people who liked to eat local protested the change of zoning from agricultural to residential that let the projects go ahead, but the desire for fenced-in backyards with swing sets and above-ground pools bulldozed all resistance. Food could always come from elsewhere, and it did: mostly Mexico, the number one producer of organic. The housing developments spawned the strip mall, an invention designed for the car and resolutely down-market, because here people had to count their pennies. The space-dwellers were living the dream of being property owners and bosses of their backyards no one could peek into, but after the down payment, the taxes, the insurance, and the monthly mortgage hit, there was not a whole lot left over for drinking in bars.

They ordered wine. Lynne switched over to white and Phil stuck with red. He tried to get comfortable on the backless bar stool. He had heard the witticism according to which a marriage is not truly mature, or tested, or God-knows-what, until it has faced and included infidelity. Like many aphorisms, it held its share of truth. But in his preoccupied state, he doubted he would be up to the test.

He joked with the barmaid about opening a fresh bottle for them.

"That's two fresh bottles," she pointed out, her nostril ring catching a wink of light. "You're asking a lot."

"The Doll's House," Phil mused. "Someone read Ibsen."

"The owner is a Mr. Dahl. I don't know how many times I've had to say that."

Exuding chic boredom, the barmaid moved off.

"I guess I've been put in my place," Phil admitted.

"I once lived in a doll's house," Lynne told him. "I can still pull off the roof and look inside."

Phil nodded. "What do you see there?"

"The characters in the drama. The people who live there."

The barmaid swept past and dropped off the check with the glasses of wine. She was all business. Lynne grabbed the bill before Phil could make a move.

"Did you have a doll house when you were a girl?"

"Yes. A play one. But not like this one. This one isn't store-bought. I helped make it."

He would not have minded some idle, introductory, flirtatious small talk, but it was not to be expected after Dr. Sheridan's soirée. He felt Lynne leading him. His obligation was to follow.

"And what are they doing inside, in there, the people who live in the house you made?"

"My husband is abusing my daughter."

Phil felt the breath leave his body. "I hope he paid for what he did."

She laughed.

"That's the first thing everyone says. Every man, I mean. It's like coming to this bar and making a crack about Ibsen. As if the proper punishment could solve anything and bring us closure, which is something I've heard about, but never seen. Talking about punishment is just a way of not thinking about the crime. Not seeing it. But since you ask, no, he didn't pay, at least not in any normal way. He got off scot-free, though he probably wouldn't say that."

She covered the bill with a twenty and the barmaid brought the change. It was closing time at the Doll's House, she informed them, and when Phil wondered why so early, the barmaid confided she had more exciting things to do elsewhere. The young, he thought, have a different concept of the service occupations: the customers are there for the pleasure of the staff. Lynne drank like a veteran, leaving the change scattered along the bar, a way of saying that this was her spot, she had paid for it, so don't try and pry me loose, no matter what time it is.

"Don't you think he should pay? Isn't it only fair for the victim?"

"I don't use the word victim."

"Funny, since the word is everywhere these days."

"Exactly. There's something passive about it that I don't like."

"How did you find out? Did your daughter tell you?"

"Goop," Lynne said. She spat the word out.

"I'm sorry. I'm afraid…"

"Goop. She kept saying *goop*. Suddenly it was there all the time, in the middle of a sentence, with things that didn't fit. Not that anything would fit with a word like that, that's not even a word. She'd be talking about our cat, and then *goop!* Suddenly, for no reason. Around that time, my husband stopped wanting me. He didn't want a woman. He couldn't function with a woman, not once he started doing what he was doing."

"I'm afraid I still don't get it," Phil said. It was unbearable to keep asking the same terrible question.

"Finally I asked my daughter what the word meant, and why she kept saying it. *I like it when the goop finally comes out because then I can stop*. That was how she told me. That was how I understood what was going on."

It was intolerable. The kind of shit you can't make up. Phil put his hand on top of Lynne's, then drew it away a moment later, as if he were part of the contamination.

"What's the matter? You didn't believe me?"

"Of course I believed you. Why wouldn't I?"

"At the time it was different. People didn't believe. Now we believe the girls."

Phil had done a magazine piece about that very subject, the great sea-change from the rush to hush to the rush to divulge. It had not been easy. The subject was nearly unapproachable, especially if the byline bore a man's name, and his editor considered that his story went astray two-thirds through, maybe in traumatic response to the subject, because at that point, he began delving into the mechanisms of belief. This is a story about social trends, not an examination of religious phenomena, the editor told him, irritated at the time Phil was taking to finish the piece. Then she asked him the question he had been waiting for: whether he had been abused as a boy, and if that heretofore hidden event might be causing him trouble with the piece. "I never thought about that," he told her, and she looked at him incredulously, since the question was at the very heart of his inquiry. Another abused kid discovering the truth late in life, the editor concluded. Phil could read the verdict in her eyes. If I had been abused, I would know it somewhere, in my flesh. Wouldn't I?

He pleaded his case. Discussing belief was necessary. How was it that people came around to accepting the existence of events they had spent so much energy denying? And not just people, individuals—the whole society they were part of and creating every day through their decisions about denial and belief. The ecology has changed, he told his editor. That's a social trend. Give me another week, I'll deliver.

The story thrust him into the lives of people—almost all of them male—whom he hated with murderous ferocity. And here he was, back again. The subject seemed to trail after him.

"Do you think there could have been some way of knowing it might happen?" he asked Lynne. "I've wondered about that."

"I ask myself the same thing every day. I guess I could have listened to my ex-boyfriend at the time. He told me not to marry him. But the ex wasn't a particularly reliable source."

"Maybe he was jealous. That would be normal."

"Well, he had me, and he didn't try to keep me. Then, a long time after he dropped me, he took me out to a bar to tell me the man I wanted to marry was a creep."

"A creep? That's a word I haven't heard for a while."

"Yeah. Well, it was a long ago."

Lynne let herself smile. She was a pretty woman, with a worn beauty that appealed to him. Phil liked women his age, unlike some men he knew who chased after young flesh and married their students, though he had none of those to choose from, and never had. He liked lived-in beauty. He wore himself hoarse telling his wife as much, though she did not seem to take it as a compliment. Once he wrote a two-minute piece that ran on the radio about that sort of beauty, hers, to be exact, and he considered his short text a brave public declaration of love that was read on the morning show, unfortunately by the traffic reporter who had a nasal voice made worse by the mobile sound system he used. The effect was nil. Amy never acknowledged his confession. He might as well have pissed in the ocean, an expression his mother loved, and that was endlessly useful in his profession.

"He published a slender volume of poetry. A chapbook. I thought that made him cool. And his family had money. Back then I liked the pretty things money can buy. I thought the world owed them to me."

"I bet his money helped him beat the charge," Phil ventured.

Lynne said nothing, and he understood it was true. It was always the thing you first liked about a person that sank you. The conversation from a table of noisy women who must have been there all evening, the only ones at the Doll's House besides them, drifted over to the bar above the music. The women were debating whether this suburb in the fields was a good place to raise a family, far from the inner city. Some of them believed that all such places had vanished. Wherever there were children, those eager consumers, there were people to sell them what they wanted, or what they didn't know they wanted until it was advertised.

A brassy voice rose above the others. "I wouldn't know about any of that. I never had children. I just had abortions." Ladies' night out in the strip mall, on the skirt of the cornfields.

"So that," Lynne summed up, "is my loss."

"But she's still with you."

"No. Well, yes. Enough to blame me."

"You know, unfortunately, that's normal."

"I do. But how do you?"

"I'm afraid I've written about it. I'm a journalist. I do what they call 'think pieces.' I have to learn a lot about very specific things. Most of the time I forget everything by the time the piece runs, but not with this subject. I'm afraid it stuck with me."

Lynne drew her hand away, though his was nowhere near hers. "I'm not going to let you write about me."

"I have absolutely no intention of doing that."

What enormous vanity, he thought—but of course she was right to assume the world was a collection of prospective subjects for a person in his position. He wondered if he could get away with not buying Lynne a return drink. The barmaid did the job for him by announcing in no uncertain terms that it was now past closing time. He promised Lynne he would make it up next time, something he was not too sure of. *What makes you think I would write about you?*

They stepped into the parking lot and surveyed the emptiness. "No one is allowed to walk here. Get in, I'll drive you to your car."

The idea was absurd, and appealed to her. In the car, his oldies but goodies CD sprung into action with the ignition. The Sims Twins launched into "Soothe Me, Baby." It took them somewhere under ten seconds to cross the distance that separated their cars, enough for the Twins to wail once or twice about their devotion. Phil stopped next to her car and shut off the engine. The love song died.

She looked at him and understood.

"Oh, no, you're going to put the moves on me."

"Right. We're going to neck in the car. Maybe even do some heavy petting."

"Thank God there's a gearshift between us."

"Sorry. But it just seemed uncivilized to say goodbye standing in a parking lot."

To prove she was right to be wary, he took her hand. It was cool and lifeless, the hand of a grief counselling soirée post-mortem.

"There. I made my move. That's as far as it goes."

"Then I'll make mine too."

She opened the door and walked the few steps to her car. Isolated, the only vehicles in a parking lot in front of a bar, they were sitting ducks for a prowling police cruiser, had there been one. But out here among the cornfields and the pig farms, there was an unwritten agreement. If you did not attract undue attention to yourself by your antics behind the wheel, you could drive home unmolested. The distance between everything made the agreement necessary, since you could not go anywhere without a car, not even to get your car, as Phil tried to prove. But at least there was always plenty of free parking.

He watched Lynne drive slowly out of the lot, miles wide and deserted except for a few down-at-the-mouth Civics that belonged to the cleaning staff. With all the strip malls and other installations to maintain, a colony of Salvadorians and Guatemalans and Hondurans had sprung up out here in the fields. Phil had even spotted a combination grocery and *pupusa* joint in one mall. As he watched her go, he felt the temptation to follow. He pictured the scene in *Chinatown* where Jack Nicholson breaks the lens of the taillight so he can follow a woman's car through the streets of Los Angeles, and learn a truth that will all but destroy him, and end the film. No thanks, not tonight. You've got troubles of your own. He put on his seat belt. As he did, he realized Lynne had not asked him a single question about his loss. She was discreet, or maybe she just didn't care.

That story that had come out two decades ago about the rush to hush and the rush to divulge for that deadline-anxious lady editor—he judged it harshly now, as he did with nearly everything he wrote. He had not gone far enough. He had not anticipated that the rush to divulge would go a step further and create crimes that had never happened, and wipe habeas corpus off the books, and turn the presumption of innocence on its head. There was only one way to protect yourself, and Phil thought he possessed it: he had no power over anyone. He did not enjoy a single moment of having sway or authority over any other person. He could not be guilty of harassment or intimidation or misconduct. It was the only sure method of self-protection: being at the bottom.

Of course there were plenty of people below him, and he did realize it. The bitterness over his disappearing career did not render him that unreasonable.

His house was miles away. Miles to go before I sleep, the poem all high school students used to learn, but in this invented landscape, there were no forks in the road, no decisions, no snowy evenings. When the automated automobile would finally be launched on mass scale, it would begin here first, on these ideal roads for it. *But she's still with you,* he had told Lynne about her daughter. An attempt at consolation, and a completely unperceptive thing to have come up with. He should have known better. He did know better. But when someone holds back information and makes you play a guessing game, you're bound to make the wrong guesses.

He played back what Lynne had told him. The girl was in a self-esteem community in a distant part of the country with more clement weather and transparent air. She was being attended to by specialists, she was being rebuilt. Presumably she was getting better. There was that much for Lynne to be happy about.

But she was not happy, not even a little. The rebuilding was taking place in the complete absence of the family. The logic was simple and stark and total. Family caused the problem, its very nature was to blame, so family had to be held at bay. Lynne was excluded from her daughter's life, a second loss added to the first. The abusive parent was isolated, she told Phil, and the innocent one as well, because in the regime of her daughter's healers, both were guilty. The one who had done nothing had enabled the abuser. That was the assumption. Guilt was systemic. According to that savage self-esteem community, somewhere in a drawer was an unwritten contract that allowed the behaviour to take place, whether anyone knew it was there or not.

Why send your daughter there? he asked. Why subject yourself to those people and their system? Lynne shook her head. He understood nothing. Her daughter's welfare, not hers, was at the heart of every decision. "Besides," Lynne added, "that place gives proven results. I know, I shopped around."

In the centre of an expanse of darkness, where productive land had not yet been converted to housing, lay a brilliantly lit set of industrial buildings surrounded by barbed wire, a Guantánamo on the plains. It was a pig farm. The high surveillance was caused by the animals' habits. They ate everything and anything, including the bodies of people who ended up on the wrong end of a business deal. These excellent places to dispose of a corpse had to be protected from people who had a corpse to dispose of. A good place to raise a family, as a young mother had maintained.

Now, as an attempt to get back in the game, Phil had proposed a piece on the new industry of grief to a new editor. It would not be commissioned, but on spec, a gamble, the only way open to him now. He had planned to compare grief in the West to other cultures and prove that the need for outside counselling when it came to mourning was part of the greater American industry of help and self-help. The smell of blood from sacred cows excited his appetite. His approach should earn him a fresh crop of haters to add to the ones he had accumulated by comparing a literary figure revered by the young to Peter Pan, the little boy who wouldn't grow up. He doubled that number with a reportage from Belgrade during the NATO bombing of 1999 which was sympathetic to the people being bombed, but who deserved it, and not sympathy, according to public opinion, because they were Serbs. Tonight was a setback. Dr. Sheridan stalled his grief investigation by refusing to let him use her and her group. He was expecting resistance, but her critique stung him: he was denying his loss by turning it into a piece for the pages of a magazine. And she was right, as she so often was. To propose writing about the industry of grief while attending a grief counselling group for his daughter who, he felt, was lost to him was an extraordinary and perverse maneuver, the kind of pulling and stretching that could injure a person. Well, why not? He had always used journalism as self-inquiry. But it did not look like this idea was going to lift him out of his slump as a journalist, which was the slump of all print media, only personalized.

At the house, his wife Amy asked the pro forma question about the women at the reception. If she wanted to check them out, he told her, if she truly was curious, she would have to come with him. And that, he knew, would never happen. Her curiosity quickly met its limits. He envied her.

"Excuse me, there's something I need to look up."

She lifted her hand and waved in his direction, dismissal or encouragement or both.

"Research away."

He quickly read the piece about the Self-Traumatized Perpetrators online, and the story was worse than he imagined. These people were traumatized by violent crimes and atrocities that did not exist, that they did not commit. So they were perpetrators of what? Self-trauma. Psychosis. There were entire populations of them. They insisted they were criminals, usually war criminals. But they weren't. What was in it for them? And more to the point, what was in it for Dana?

He tried to engage with her disorders. He was proud of his effort and understanding. But he was reaching a limit.

He decided it was early enough to go down the hallway and knock on her door.

"Access denied," Dana called from behind it. "Again."

Phil opened the door and walked into Dana's room. This evening it felt like a sickroom, the way the air hung like a damp curtain, more intense than a couple hours ago. How had that happened? Anorexics had a telltale smell that came from their bodies consuming their own flesh in the absence of nourishment, but it wasn't that, at least he didn't think so. It was indifference—indifference to her body, unwashed, uncared for, the same clothes every day. The papers scattered around her on the bed, the desk, the floor, a packrat's nest. They added to the disorder. They were the disorder. He imagined her as one of those itinerants on a subway grate, covered in matted newspapers, back in the city Amy had wanted to leave behind.

"You're back," she deduced.

"I read about the perpetrators," he announced. "Just now."

"You're fast. Too fast, maybe?"

"Well, everything's online."

"So I hear."

"You're not claiming to be a perpetrator, are you?"

Phil could be so smart at times, but he was blinded by his worries about her. She found him touching, he figured, but irritating. He wanted her to explain, and she didn't like explanations.

"Do you become everything you read and write about?"

"No, thank God." He allowed himself to smile. "The guy who wrote this, he thinks these people have no future."

"Their disorder has no future," she corrected him. "That's not the same thing. But it's true, he doesn't like them very much. Neither do you, probably. But that's not the point." She paused. "How was your group outing?"

"The grief counsellor threw a party. You can imagine the atmosphere."

"You went to a grief group because of me? I'm not dead yet, or don't you know that?"

"I went for me, sweetie, not for you. I get to do that sometimes."

Dana lifted her head. It seemed to demand a lot of energy from her. The order of the papers on her bed and desk, he saw, had been reshuffled. She lay on the bed with her shoes on. Why does she need shoes, Phil thought, she hardly goes out.

She smiled her apprentice predator's smile, and never had

the truth appeared so blatant to Phil: troubled people are master manipulators. They have to be, since they are manipulated by their disorders. They learn from them. They are apprentices to the master builder.

"No one can hear you scream in outer space," she told her father.

"*Alien*, 1979. Sigourney Weaver, Hollywood's tallest actress, plus a monster. I missed it."

"Ever wonder why no one can hear you scream in outer space?"

Phil shook his head. This was a night for guessing games. He had been burned by his wrong guesses so he gave this question a pass.

"There's no air," his daughter told him. "No air, so no sound. You need air to carry sound."

"The things you know that I don't."

"I got it online."

Everything was online, it was a giant flea market, and you didn't have to leave your room. Lynne lived in a doll house, or so she said. Maybe he was living in a spaceship with an alien who was his daughter, and the energy from her static state radiated outward from her room and devoured everything in the house, starting with him, the most vulnerable target. Disorder was a force field.

He bent down and picked up one of the three-by-five cards she had bought at a vintage shop. "How goes the work?"

"You know what it's like. Good one day, not so good the next."

"We're in the same business. I'm glad about that."

Dana did have a vocation for history, what her kindly professor had called an obsession. She had given herself entirely to the Ukrainian famine that Stalin had engineered in the early

1930s, which had killed millions. Three-by-five cards were strewn across her bed like islands. Was Phil a model for her work? He hoped not, but somewhere he had to be part of it. He could be dismayed at so much work for nothing, but he could not be surprised. Maybe it wasn't work. Maybe it was therapy, except that therapy was meant to make a person get better, and he did not see how these cards were doing that.

The latest installment of her chronicles—that was her word for what she did—explored what people ate when there was nothing to eat. Nothing to eat on purpose, since famine is created by humans. Dana studied the inventive techniques and survivor cunning of the Ukrainian peasants who were starving to death in the breadbasket of Europe.

He put down the card exactly where it had been. That was one of her rules: her order must not be disturbed.

"This is good stuff. With what's going on between Russia and Ukraine these days, you're in business."

"We're Russians. That puts us on the side of the fomenters of genocide. How do you like that?"

"We're not exactly Russians. Your great-grandfather on my side fled Russia to save his skin."

"We're still guilty. We enabled genocide."

"*We* means you too?"

"Of course. Don't be stupid."

He was being stupid. Dana felt intensely guilty, though about what, he did not know. Maybe it was the face of self-loathing, or melancholy, though no one used that word anymore. Maybe hers was a transient disorder. He had a colleague in the business whose daughter once burned her arms with cigarettes, and now she was a wife, happily married, with a job, the mother of two little girls. Why not Dana?

"I like reading your stuff."

"That's not the point, liking it or not."

He went out and closed the door to the sickroom.

I am only as happy as my unhappiest child.

That Dr. Sheridan mantra was a lot more intriguing than the one about not making yourself feel worse, which he had quoted for Lynne's benefit at the wine table. How many unhappy children did a person have to have? Apparently, just one. One was enough to colour the landscape. The superlative was there only for effect. *I am only as happy as my unhappy child.*

Phil walked into the kitchen. The night was proving to be endless. He stood dangling there in the room reputed to produce domestic contentment. In the kitchen was a little table, a material souvenir of their early years. The table comfortably sat just two, and he and Amy used to eat breakfast there when they had time to share and wanted only each other as company, and the girls obliged by sleeping in or watching television. On the table lay a book he did not remember having seen, a graphic novel by an author with a French name, Beauchard. Phil never bothered with graphic novels. They contained more graphics than novel, and he was a narrative guy. This one was called *Epileptic.* It had a lurid black-and-white cover. He opened it.

And understood. The book had to have come from Megan. The daughter without the disorder. *You have forgotten me. Sooner or later you will pay for your neglect.*

Phil turned the spreads. A boy was telling the tale of his brother who suffered from severe epilepsy. There were pages and pages of nightmare depictions of seizures as the brother without the disease tried to imagine what it would be like to live with the brain of his brother with the disease. Phil put the book under his arm. He would read it tonight. It was his duty to Megan.

He went to the door that led to the finished basement. When Megan announced she wanted to live down there, Phil was comforted. At last, typical teenage behaviour, happily normal. He was glad to pay for the renovations that separated off a room for her from the jumble of domestic machinery, installed a proper window and turned the downstairs exit that was no more than an escape route into a functioning door. "You're pushing her into having a sex life," Amy told him. "Maybe she's not even ready for that. But now she can have a different boy over every night and we won't even know." Phil smiled at his wife's fantasy. "Not if she takes after her mother." That set off Amy's anger, as he knew it would. "This isn't about us," she insisted.

Phil stood at the top of the stairs. "Thanks for the book," he called down to the basement.

Megan answered from deep in the house, some kind of positive acknowledgement, he hoped, though he did not hear the words.

Dana and Megan, his girls. He thought of Lynne's story. The abuse of her daughter made him feel sullied and violated, for her and for himself. And then for his daughters, as if it had happened to them too. Another person's story could hurt you, and that hurt could travel through time. He could hardly bring himself to say the words: *sexually abused*. Though the real word was *raped*. The word *rape* was out of the legal vocabulary, and he considered that a shame. Of course he understood the reasoning behind the change, and was okay with it if it helped bring more justice to more women who had been forced into doing something they did not want to. But there was something primitive and elemental about the word *rape* that grabbed people and shocked them. It was a word from the battlefields of the recent ethnic wars, and from World War II Berlin. He had investigated that issue in print too, the rape camps of Bosnia that existed, then disappeared, then returned to exist again, during the middle of the 1990s. Whatever else, whatever the truth of the claims of the propaganda wars, when you wrote that word, people felt the assault, they felt the pain in the fabric of their bodies.

His wife, whose body he cherished, had been one of those women. *Was* one of those women, and would always be. He could hardly stand what she had told him, early on, when they were lovers starting out. There were many things in a marriage that you could not think about every day.

A woman once said to him that no doubt he had done the same thing: forced someone into non-consensual sex. She was one of those spray-painting graffiti sisters who had defiled the wall of the Social Sciences Building with their slogans. When he protested, she assured him, "Oh, it's not necessarily your fault. She probably didn't feel she could tell you she didn't want to." "Great," he retorted. "Where does that leave me? Some of the time I didn't want to either." Back then he'd been self-righteous and dismissive, but he was no rapist, no one had to be in those days of liberation—another mindless thing men said. But when Amy told him how she had given in to a man she did not want, the intimidation, the physical overwhelming—there were so many words for it and no one word fully summed up what could happen—that woman's accusation, a generation old, returned. By then he was less defensive, and he recognized what she had said for what it was. It was not a personal accusation. It did not call for refutation. He was being made to stand in the rapist's shoes, and consider his own behaviour and where it stood in the power relations between men and women. The next step was not difficult to take, and it led to a question that could not be answered, let alone asked. He wondered how much sex with his wife had been non-consensual. Maybe that was the message she was sending when she told him about that incident from years before they met, out of the blue, with no seeming connection to anything they were experiencing together.

But, of course, there was a connection. *Don't you ever do that to me.* Unless, he speculated on a somewhat brighter note, she was testing his affection for her. In which case, apparently he passed the test, at least at the time.

Now Phil wondered if that wasn't the beginning of the slump. The way he didn't know and couldn't know if the woman he wanted wanted him or whether she was just tolerating his wanting, if the moral high ground he thought he occupied was just a shelter for the rapist in him. He could not find the words to describe his dilemma to Amy. He did not think those words existed, at least not between them as they were now. *Have you ever really wanted me?*—can a man say that to his wife? The question was loaded with accusation. It was unsayable. The slump became his daily companion. That was how he thought of it, to himself, and with his friend Bruno, a *slump*, a term from baseball when a hitter who was expected to hit stopped hitting. A mediocre player was not subject to slumps because no one expected much from him. He had been a reliable hitter, but he had not found a way to break out of his slump. He needed a mojo or a black-cat bone or Love Potion Number Nine, some kind of magic formula that fought loss.

What he really needed was a new project, a piece that had an intimate connection with him, and that he had the authority to talk about. Unfortunately, the trade he had worked in for years was in a slump too. And every story that concerned him deeply enough led him back to Dana, and he did not know how to write about her. A shame, since she was the only subject that interested him.

Phil carried the book into the bedroom. Amy looked in his direction and read the title.

"Aren't we busy enough with the diseases we already have?"

Phil did not expect her to be happy that a graphic novel about epilepsy was coming into the bedroom late in the evening. He should have slipped it into the drawer of the bedside table instead of exhibiting it.

"Megan left it for us."

Amy let out a great breath of air. "I can't take any more."

"It's not a bad thing. It means she's attentive to her sister. But that we aren't being attentive to her."

"How could it be any other way?" Amy glanced at the cover of the book, then averted her eyes showily. "Don't let me see it, I'll get bad dreams. Anyway, I'm not the right demographic for graphic novels."

"Then don't look, dear."

He settled in next to her as she turned off her bedside light, then he opened the first page of the book. Here was Megan's loss, depicted by a stranger from another country who had experienced the same dismay. Your sister is your flesh and blood, your other, she is helpless and visited by monsters, it is worse than having a parent with a disease because a child defines herself against her parents. Her sister is supposed to be her closest ally in the common front against them. That was the book's message. Megan was in a house where she had no sister, and no parents either because they were devoured by that non-sister and the impotent worry about her that sucked in all their attention like the black hole of a sci-fi movie.

If you're a parent, you'd better listen to that.

Phil had had a good run at his job for a couple of decades, maybe more. He liked looking for trouble, and he was good at finding it. He really didn't have to work too hard; he let his nature run free. That consisted in positioning himself on the other side of his readers' expectations. That tickled his editor Susan—"tickled," that was the word she used—because she considered his pieces works of youthful provocation, even if he was older than she was. The fall of the Berlin Wall as seen from the German Democratic Republic, also known as East Germany, by its citizens leery of being embraced to death by capitalist arms. Yeltsin's vodkacracy and the coup he staged against himself in order to consolidate power. The young men of Serbia in the early 1990s who had ten addresses, all false, to avoid Milošević's army. And the Serbs in Sarajevo who refused to leave the neighbourhoods where they lived harmoniously with Muslims and Catholics, and who were punished for their tolerance by their brothers who were conducting the siege and raining down shells on their apartment blocks every day for years.

Post-Soviet Europe provided Phil with a good run, but it was over. So many subjects were out of bounds now. He could not camp out on a reserve in the wilderness and report on the epidemic of male violence, even if it was true. Political correctness forbade it. Some conflict zones were so unpredictable and dangerous that it would be suicidal to go there. The headless ghost of Daniel Pearl trailed after him like a shroud when he got big ideas about certain hot spots. And some stories were just too terrible to have two sides, and he did not want to do advocacy journalism. There was one more factor he preferred to avoid. He was getting a little too old for this sport, and his editors let him know as much in their unsubtle way.

And with Dana's ever-changing condition, he could not disappear from the house for long periods of time to hunt down stories about other people's traumatic situations. In the self-blame that every parent engages in, he wondered whether his trips when she was young had some determining negative effect. Logically, they did not. Megan had not suffered from his absences. But Megan was not Dana. When he was in Moscow during the beginning of the Yeltsin era, he had a dream that had him grabbing the first plane home—almost. Every detail was as plain and terrifying today as it had been when he awoke in a distant cousin's apartment next to the Bely Dom, a couple hundred metres from where Yeltsin had taken his theatrical stand on top of a tank, and the Russians, eager believers as they have always been, ate up the act with a shovel. Phil was walking along a street called Hertzina, though the name had been changed since. It was bordered by buildings painted in the pastel colours of the Maria Theresa style, one harmonious length of street a block long in the overall soul-denying ugliness of the Russian capital. He felt a moment of pleasure, but the truce of that temporary beauty was designed to deliver him to the next sight, a park the Muscovites had turned into a garbage dump, since the city had stopped picking up their trash. He realized that everything had been leading him to this spot—maybe it was the true reason for his trip. It was to see this one thing. On top of the heap of garbage, more than a heap, a small mountain because he looked down on Phil from Olympian heights, sat a boy. He had the flat, square features of a Russian, though it was an old man's face on a boy's body, and his straight, colourless hair was plastered against his forehead, as if he were ill and sweating out his fever. He was as pale as a corpse. He gazed down upon Phil from the heights of his garbage mountain, the king of his castle of trash, and said nothing, though the air buzzed with the unspoken question of why Phil had abandoned him.

The boy's reproach buzzed like a wasp caught in a jar. It woke him up, that and the fact he could offer no answer.

The character was a boy, and Phil assumed it was himself on top of that heap of trash, the aged child with the wary, resentful weasel face shared by so many men on the Moscow streets. He hated every minute he spent in that place, though the trip was among the most productive of his career, and brought in a respectable fee.

Then the truth came to him, slicing through his faulty first interpretation: the boy was Dana. *Why have you forsaken me?* He told the dream, and his first and subsequent interpretations of it, to Anne Sheridan.

"You've said it all."

"But it wasn't really my fault. I was away for work."

"Fault—that's not what the dream is saying. The dreamer is the one bringing the feeling of guilt."

They sat in silent meditation in the shelter of the white noise from Dr. Sheridan's dehumidifier. That session was time well spent.

The Moscow dream was rich in terrifying interpretations, but it did not get Phil any closer to finding a subject for a magazine piece that would let him make a living, and save him from leaning on Amy's hefty salary as the head public relations officer for a hospital. He was beginning to think his run was over; at nearly fifty, he was over the hill. It wasn't just because there were no more newspapers. Reading was reading, and people had to read, whether it was on a miniscule screen or paper that smudged their fingers.

45

He was paper-nostalgic like most people his age, and in the conversations with his editors he brandished the studies that showed even young people liked to receive information important to them via hard copy. The more essential it was to them, the more they wanted it in a medium they could hold in their hands. His strategy was the equivalent of talking himself out of existence, since he was implying that the information he had to offer was non-essential.

Phil's boyhood had been dedicated to paper, and the timely delivery of it into the right hands. He had two paper routes on two different days for two different papers. Paper put him into contact with men, and showed him their world, the nurturing and the threatening sides. When the Burlington local stopped at the station in the meagre shopping district in his neighbourhood as evening fell, it would bring the early edition of the *Sun-Times*. Even before the train ground to a halt with that metal-on-metal sound he loved, the conductors would be throwing off bales of newspapers, bound tightly with steel wire, onto the platform. The ink on page one was practically still wet. Phil's job was to carry the bales from the platform to the news agency that sold the papers, not far, a few hundred feet, but long enough to need gardening gloves to protect his fingers from the wire. The bales were heavy for a skinny boy, too heavy, but they taught him how to resist pain. Once he lugged his burden to the news agency, the clerk handed him a pair of wire-cutters. It took Phil only once to learn that the wire leapt up into your face when you cut it if you did not hold it down with your gloved hand. The news agency sold newspapers along with any number of products whose uses he dimly understood from having touched them in the drawer of his father's bedside table. He was a boy among men, and he understood he must not turn his back on them. No one warned him. He figured it out from their eyes. This was the beginning of his career as a journalist: the romance of the trains, the conductors in their uniforms smelling of cigarettes from the smoking car, the noise the bales of paper made as they hit the asphalt platform, the train pulling away with the rusty sound of steel wheels that would severe your legs if you got in their way, the urgency to get the papers to the news agency because after all this was the news, people needed to know, that's why there were papers, those daily sheets that had taught him how to read, starting with the box scores in the sports section. People holding sheets of paper with fresh ink that stained their hands—that was the real story. They would read the stories and talk trash about what the writers said, but trash or not, no one could afford not to read the papers, it would be like cutting yourself off from society, a blatant act of self-exclusion, an admission that you were an ignoramus or a hermit. The news agency clerk gave Phil a tip for bringing the papers from the train, and Phil could feel the man sizing him up. The clerk was a pervert but Phil didn't mind. He wanted money in his pockets, and his parents did not give him an allowance.

The opportunities to do his job were shrinking, and those that remained went to journalists younger and more in tune with the culture of complaint, who could boast of something in their autobiographies that gave them a moral leg up that Phil didn't have. Or didn't have anymore. When he was a boy, he was part of an oppressed minority with all the prestige and sexiness that status imparted, he had family members slaughtered in the killing fields, but unfortunately those fields were in Europe and they didn't count anymore. He was lumped together with the oppressors. He had become white, something he never was when he was younger.

47

In 2007, he created a project based in the former Yugoslavia to try to answer that charge. He wrote a story and accompanied it with footage on YouTube that invited viewers to look into the blue, blue eyes of a woman who had been held captive in a roofless grain silo in Bosnia and raped repeatedly at the convenience of men with guns—she refused to call them soldiers, and insisted she did not know what side they were on. *Look at the blue-eyed refugees and the fair-haired torture victims, they exist too. History happens everywhere.* He won a minor humanitarian prize for his document, and even received proper payment, but no one got the point he was trying to make. Or if they did, they wouldn't admit it.

Being underemployed, he had time to spend in Dana's room after Amy went to work. Dana would insist that access was denied, and he would enter. It was their game, permitted and denied, denied and permitted, with always the same results, a good sign because self-humour was present. There was something in her room he needed to learn. On rough days, it was not easy to keep company with her disorders. You're being cruel by encouraging her, Amy accused. She did not have the stomach for the ride. "I'm engaging with the illness. I won't be intimidated by it. I'm accompanying her." Amy shook her head. "I can't separate them. Dana and whatever problem she has. Bipolar. Anorexia. Borderline personality syndrome. Hysteria, even if they say it doesn't exist. Possession by demons—I don't know anymore!" Amy was on the edge of tears. She and her daughter were women, and Dana was refusing to be a woman like she was, or a woman at all, of any kind. She was rejecting her, she was hurting her, and she had a right to her pain.

"It's easier for me," Phil told her. "If you don't mind, I'll continue."

"And if I do mind?"

What he once thought of as the sickroom became his reading room. He was happy to see he had a writer under his roof, and he told her so. Usually he read standing or leaning on her desk with papers and file cards in his hand. Once he sat down on her bed. The next minute he was back on his feet. The bed was vibrating with energies that threw him off like a rodeo bull.

A number of years back, Phil had written about the ordeals of his refugee family, and how they echoed through the genealogy in the new world. He called the piece "Stalin and Me." Logically, Dana could not have read it. She was too young, her level would not have been up to the challenge of reading and understanding a five-thousand-word magazine piece. As Hitler marched on Moscow with promises to raze the city to the ground and turn the site into a lake, Phil's cousins on his father's side, Clara and Walter, were classified as "non-productives" and evacuated. It was not evacuation, they were deported, and "non-productive" meant they were ideologically untrustworthy. The authorities put them on a train to Kazakhstan, that great dumping ground for undesirable elements in Stalin's Russia, the ones he did not have time or bullets to kill. It was wartime, the trainload of shifty elements was shunted onto a sidetrack every time a military transport came through, and Clara and Walter and their comrades took a month to make the trip that now took several hours by plane.

Phil wondered how they survived. What did they eat? How did they wash, if they did? Where did they go to the toilet?

Obviously, they had lived to tell the tale through Phil, and his words. They were resilient before the word came into circulation. They made a kind of tea, it turned out, or thin soup out of carrot skins. They bought the carrots as they waited on a sidetrack, where peasants would appear out of nowhere to sell what they stored in their root cellars. Phil had seen this arrangement before, in the tropics. There was a bridge on the Pan-American Highway in Costa Rica that had lost one of its two lanes, and the result was a line-up of cars and trucks kilometres long. Food stands sprung up along the roadside, there was music and beer and rum and the opportunity to quench thirsts of all kinds.

As he read his daughter's famine chronicles, he wondered if he was somehow at the root of her traumatic interest—if it was all his fault. He went to his archives. "Stalin and Me" was published years ago, when she was in grade school. Logically, he argued with himself, he could not be responsible for the way her disorder attached itself to this distant event few knew about in North America. She would have to be reading at an adult level at age eight. She had grown up in abundance, and never met anyone from her grandparents' generation, who were all safely in the ground. When he was a kid, concentration camp survivors often came over for dinner. They walked through the door and immediately burst into tears. When they left, they were still crying, despite their full bellies that could never be full enough. Phil made it his business to shelter Dana and Megan from those injuries.

But something had happened despite his apparent protection. Something had been communicated. History was a sieve. He was not free of blame.

Maybe ancestral memory did exist. Dana remembered events she had never experienced. It was a tropism of her imagination. Another word for disorder, or aesthetic choice, or whatever attracted a certain person to a certain subject.

The things people ate to stay alive in his daughter's chronicles fascinated him and gave him nausea in equal parts. He supposed that was the point: to suppress the appetites. The meals could not have been very tasty, starting with hedgehogs, the smaller, more timid European version of the porcupine. From Dana, he learned they were easily enough caught, especially by a desperate, starving person who, self-taught, would singe them to pull off the quills. Then they could be skinned and grilled: all dark meat, and served with something called orach that he had never heard of. Inappropriate thoughts intruded to protect him from what he was reading. A cookbook. Dana could publish a cookbook of famine recipes. Who knows what today's marketplace might embrace?

"Where did they find that stuff?"

"In the fields. Foraging. In the forest. You'd have to know the landscape."

"You're not making anything up?"

"I don't need to. You wouldn't believe the shit that happened. A girl could age from lack of food and look like an old woman overnight. People ate nightingales."

"Those birds? They sing so beautifully."

"I've never heard one in real life. But I listened to their song online. Nice. And I like the name. Night and gale. A dark and stormy night."

"I'll take you on a trip one day to listen to them."

Her chronicles contained more than misery. There was strangeness, poetry, eating nightingales and hedgehogs, not just rats and mice and snails, though no doubt they would figure in the story too. They would show up sooner or later when things got really bad. Dana had an aesthetic sense. No two more different animals could be imagined, and she brought them together: the nightingale and the hedgehog. It sounded like a fable. She was both creatures.

Her disorder might become a profession. Long before autism turned into the great wave it was now, a girl from Boston named Temple Grandin who could not bear to be touched figured out a revolutionary way to stream animals into the slaughterhouse so they would go willingly, peacefully, serene and Zen, their meat all the tastier for it. Out in cattle country, her method was recognized and adopted throughout the profession. She wrote a book about it, *Thinking in Pictures*, and between the book and her patent on the slaughterhouse method she became a millionaire. She went on tv—a girl with an apparently crippling disorder. Why not Dana?

He stepped out of her room and closed the door carefully, exhausted by his manic hopes for her. He needed somewhere safe to go. He did not have a woodshop in the basement where he turned out knickknacks, or in the garage because they didn't have one, just a carport. He ought to get out more often and stop engaging in psycho-tourism under his own roof, as Amy called it. He was doing their daughter more harm than good, it was collusion, why couldn't he understand how indecent playing with their daughter's pain was? It was painful for her too, though she had given up expecting any consideration from her husband, now that he was the principle partner in the relationship that contained only him and Dana. His training in journalism made him a vulture.

Lately, out of nowhere, or nowhere he could see, Amy had begun insisting that what they needed was a bigger house, though it would be beyond their means with his economic slump. And their needs as a family too, with their daughters moving out sooner or later, bringing the downsizing couples their age faced. Dana should have her own wing, she declared, and at first Phil did not understand. He thought *wings* as in flying, spreading her wings. Amy made her meaning clear. She could not respond to his advances when their daughter was crouching in her room at the end of the hall, making symbolic war on womanhood.

He did not think a bigger house would solve anything, and he made the mistake of telling her so. She counterattacked.

Her daughter's disorder had eroded her libido, Amy told him. She no longer knew what her body was for. It belonged to another woman she could not recognize. Anyway, your affection for me, she informed Phil, is pro forma. You don't really feel it. I can tell. I don't even need woman's intuition.

Phil had a colleague, a fellow melancholy journalist whose depressive state managed to be convivial, a cynic but not immoral, a man whose conquests inevitably dumped him. His name was Bruno, and he was Phil's best friend. Phil loved hearing his stories, it seemed incredible the number of women who fell into his arms because, as Amy pointed out over and over, "The guy has a real problem with women." What could his problem be? He was deeply sad behind his cynicism, the most transparent of disguises. Phil saw that melancholy and felt protective of Bruno, and when he told Amy that, she asked him if he was out of his mind. Bruno was a man's man who could not keep his women, and maybe didn't want to. If he had one moral weakness, and Phil knew he had to have more than one, it was that women weren't real to him. Emotionally real. And this from a guy who was a model of empathy when it came to writing about one difficult human situation after another.

Phil entrusted him with the story of his soirée at Dr. Sheridan's and the drink at the Doll's House. He had heard nothing from Lynne after that first evening. The business with the goop would not leave him alone. The fact that the perpetrator had gone unpunished, the injustice of that, and the sense there was something more behind the sudden ease with which Lynne told him about the abuse. He indulged in some magical thinking. I'm good at finding things out. I know how to research. I'll find out how the husband got away with it. I'll finally get him charged.

That was the kind of fantasy that kills marriages, and ends lives. The admission of the burn victim to the physicians called in to repair the damage: the bed was on fire when I laid down on it. The perfect antidote for magical thinking, Phil knew, was hard-headed Bruno.

The man lived in an apartment of striking squalor; he was clearly punishing himself for some past misconduct. The place was sub-student. Even a bunch of male undergrads would have attempted a few embellishing touches and put up a few posters. He loved coming here and finishing off a bottle of big-shouldered red wine, unaccompanied by so much as a handful of black olives. Here were a few hundred square feet of no domestic care.

Phil related the events in Lynne's doll house, and how the abuser had not paid, and the offence to his sense of justice.

"What was his MO?"

"His what?"

"What did he actually do, in detail?"

"You think I could ask her that?"

"How are you going to catch him if you don't know his MO? You have to know what makes him tick, what his routine is, what he can't live without—if you want to catch him."

Phil's crime show vocabulary finally caught up. He shook his head. "I guess I'm not committed enough."

"Yes, you are. She made you forget to ask the right questions. Go back and find out."

"What got me is that she assumed I didn't believe her. Of course I believe her. You read my piece about hush and divulge."

"I did, but maybe she didn't. I always figured you were talking about yourself."

"If I was, I didn't know it."

There were some people Phil could take anything from. Bruno was one of those. He was right to assume that if a person were writing about that subject, it was wholly or partly out of a spirit of self-investigation. But that didn't mean the thing hadn't happened. It was a philosophical position. Though he was no fan of the discredited recovered memory syndrome, he could not deny that something that could have happened had not happened.

Bruno filled their glasses. Phil turned the bottle and read the label. The wine was from Alicante, a region unknown to him, but much better than grief soirée Rioja.

"This has something to do with your daughter, then."

That was why he treasured Bruno, besides his careless domestic space: the way he made leaps. He was like a good shrink in that ability to piece together the seemingly detached parts of a man's life.

"That would be hard to deny. Everything does."

"No, Phil, be more specific. Is it the abuse? Or belief? Ask yourself."

"I don't know. Something in the woman's attitude. Something detached."

"Maybe she didn't want to tell you everything on the first date."

They inhabited the possibilities that branched out under the influence of Spanish *tinto*. Another reason for his friendship:

he and Bruno could easily accept silence together, and for more than a few seconds.

"She didn't seem overly concerned that her husband was never charged for what he did."

"You want him to be charged. You want it more than she does. You want to rescue the damsel in distress so she will fall in love with you. She is in distress, yes. But you know that in abuse cases everyone is a little complicit."

"Even the victim?"

"I don't like that word," he told Phil.

"Neither does she. I was surprised. I don't get it. Because 'victim' means the person isn't at fault, and we want to blame everybody? You're saying that the woman's little girl was complicit?"

"I am not saying that. We're both fathers, even if you're a better one than I am. No, it's because of victim culture. The departments of victimology at the universities. It's everywhere. It's thread-bare. I'm sick of it."

"You're just saying that because you want to be a victim, but no one will let you."

"In my case, it's a private affair."

"You can't be a victim in private. You need a stage."

Bruno poured more wine into Phil's glass, though he hadn't drunk from it yet.

"You're the expert researcher. You could find this guy. You could uncover new facts that would make the charges stick. But you would not be paid—unless you wrote a story about it with yourself as the avenger."

"She expressly forbade me from writing about her."

"Ah, you are in that deeply… So you have come here to confess. Please feel free to begin. Your secret's safe with me."

"There is no secret."

"Ah! A shame. Then this is a pre-confession."

They laughed and drank from their overflowing glasses. Time spent with Bruno was balm on his heart, time without responsibility except to the sacrament of friendship. Bruno pro-posed they move on to another bottle, since the Alicante had not been full to start with. Providentially, he did have one, but somewhere between the opening of the Alicante the night before and the present moment, he had misplaced the corkscrew. His apartment managed to be both sparsely furnished and loaded down with objects with no apparent purpose outside of concealing corkscrews. Bruno turned to what he called the farmer's method: jamming the cork down the neck of the bottle with a screwdriver. There was some spillage, but he avoided collateral damage by carrying out the operation in the bathtub. He obviously had some experience with the method.

Later, Phil gathered up his car keys as Bruno wished him no encounters with the police. Phil tried to embrace his friend, but the results were awkward. Bruno was a friend, his conversations could be brilliant, but physically, the man was impossible to get close to. That was why he could not keep his women. He was all spines and thorns without the tenderness to compensate for the scratches.

Phil sat in the car and evaluated the situation. He had driven with one eye closed before, and hated the experience. It was too late to turn around and knock on Bruno's door and ask to sleep in one of his busy, rumpled beds, though Bruno would have been glad to take him in, he would have been triumphant, a blow struck against the institution of marriage. It was time to invoke the god of drunks and fools. The Russians had one, and appealed to him often—he assumed that god was male.

As he drove and prayed, he thought of those horrible Moscow drinking stories from the Yeltsin days, when getting smashed and passing out was considered a man's patriotic duty to his motherland. The stories might have been horrible, but they suited the purpose of the piece he was writing at the time, in the years after the Berlin Wall fell. The story was designed to depict the new Wild East, the everyday savagery that ruled Russia after Gorbachev. Phil had gotten more than he'd bargained for in Moscow, and not just the garbage heap dream that could have been fuelled by what Freud called recent and indifferent material, though these were not sights any person could be indifferent to. The pair of rat-faced, furtive men stripping a corpse of its clothing behind a bush in a park as he walked to an assignation with his translator and fixer Tatiana Pocherstnik. Rigor mortis was making the men's work difficult, and Phil stopped to watch their efforts. One of the men looked up and shouted at him. He turned to Tatiana. "They are saying that he told them to take his clothes when he died, since he no longer has need of them."

As they walked to an interview for his piece "See You in the Next Obituary," Tatiana bombarded him with tales of the crude things men did when they drank. She had clearly been abused by alcohol, or by someone who abused it. "In the Ukraine, but they are like us in this way, three men sat down to drink in a park. They had the kind of vodka with the paper stopper, when you take it off you can't put it back. So you must finish it. But first, when they were still sober, these men made a solemn pact: the first man who passed out, he would be eaten by the other two. Everyone signed—they could all read and write, they were members of the intelligentsia. They drank, night fell, first one bottle, then another, and finally one of the men fell off the park bench. The other two waited. Maybe it was a momentary loss of consciousness, maybe he would return to himself. But no. The two men who remained, who had become very hungry by then, the ways drinkers do, built a fire with wood scraps they found in the park and solemnized the agreement. They were condemned for murder and cannibalism and executed."

They were reaching the place of his next interview. There was not much time. Phil wanted to know: did these men offer a defense?

"They produced the contract. But the State Prosecutor rejected it."

Tatiana loved telling these stories, and she had a treasure house of them designed to shock the Western gullibility of the various men she worked for. In her world view, all Westerners were naïve. The Russian ability to live in squalor and deprivation proved their moral superiority. Phil tested his faculties and found he was now able to drive with both eyes open, and not have the road splinter into two sharp fragments going opposite ways. Why do people do this to themselves, he wondered, what sort of self-punishment is it? He homed in on his street, a crescent-shaped arrangement of streetlights set off against the last remaining cornfield. Tatiana's stories were like the *Decameron*. They ensured safe passage on a perilous journey through the plague lands.

When he finally left Moscow, the most hateful city he had spent time in, Tatiana told him, "You are no prince, but you are charming." That word play was her reaction to the bottle of Chanel No. 5 he had given her as a gift, paid for by the magazine's expense account that accompanied the honorarium. To her, it was such an extravagant gift it brought tears to her eyes. "We must see each other again," she said with sudden urgency. "You must come back to me." But the garbage heap dream kept him far from Moscow, and if any of the players from "See You in the Next Obituary" had survived, they would have rubbed him out on his first day back.

Phil eased into his driveway. Don't you ever do this to me again, he warned the steering wheel.

A few days later, Dana's wandering nature jumped to a new object. Phil had no talent for drawing, and if Amy did, she had kept it hidden. Dana must have pulled hers out of the air, where apparently genius resides, in waiting.

From under her bed, from a shoebox, a portfolio, new hiding places, dozens of sheets of paper materialized. They had probably been there all along. Phil had access just about any time he wanted, but it was never more than superficial.

His daughter was now an anime cartoon artist. Her drawings showed characters in bold confrontation in close-up, faces inches apart, in a shouting match, or so it looked to him, but there were no dialogues to help out. They seemed to be men and women locked in conflict, and he immediately thought that these were portraits of Amy and him, and he wondered if he and his wife looked that way to her, big wide exaggerated eyes and nearly featureless faces. A minute later he saw it differently. The clownish, immature Pierrot faces were neither male nor female. All the panels were close-ups, but when there was a section of body, it was lithe, slender, undetermined. Amy's and his body were not like this.

"This is something new. I thought you were into the famine."

"I have room for more than one interest."

What the famine said and what anime said seemed incompatible. For the journalist in him, the first was tragic fact, human suffering knowingly engineered by a twentieth-century demon, something he could relate to and knew about. The second was a flimsy, faddish product of Japanese pop culture, a celebration of superficiality.

"I'm sorry, I don't get the Japanese stuff."

"That's not the point, if it comes from Japan."

"When I was a kid, all the monster movies came from there. They were all secretly about the atom bomb, though we didn't know it at the time."

Dana put on her under-impressed teenager look, though her teenage years were behind her. The mushroom cloud was a distant story. A dozen holocausts had come and gone since Hiroshima.

He set a page on Dana's bed and picked up another. The panels were nearly identical in their portraiture and mood. Without a story, they did not say much to him. He didn't know how to read images without words—no doubt a weakness of his. He could assimilate a graphic novel, but not this.

"How many of these do you have?"

"I don't know. A hundred, maybe."

"Imagine what you could do with them."

Dana stared at him blankly. *Do with them?* They were doing, already. That should be obvious. For her father, everything had to produce. Then he should be happy. These pictures were producing.

"Maybe you could send them out somewhere."

"I am."

"Really? That's great. Who to?"

"A friend. We trade. One day we're going to make our own book."

"What's it going to be about?"

"I don't know yet. Whatever we decide, together."

The trail ended there. Her intention was too fragile to put into words. Dana had the artist's superstition when it came to talking about her work. Phil's job involved getting people to talk, and say things they did not plan to. His training fell apart when it came to his daughter. He wanted to know if the friend she was sending her drawings to was a boy or a girl, and if they met face to face, and where. But he had pried enough for one day. He was exhausted by the chase.

Summer settled over the cornfields, the winds were calm and free of the smell from the pig farms that visited the families who allowed the evening air to come into their air-conditioned houses. Phil was on a mission to track down *morita* chilies for his version of red *mole*. He decided to try the Latino grocery that doubled as a *pupusa* outlet. A *pupusa* was an empanada by a different name. Service industries sprung up where they were needed, sometimes before people realized they needed them. Out here among the fields, with the strip malls and hotels with giant conference rooms and mammoth grocery chains, everything outsized, dwarfing the customer, personnel was required to stock the shelves and change the sheets on the beds and mop up the spilled drinks after hours. The people who did these essential tasks came from Honduras, El Salvador, Guatemala. Without them, the economy could not function. Like everybody else, these people needed to eat, and they wanted to eat the things they liked. If you knew the right strip mall, you could find excellent *moritas* just as good as the ones in the Latino *barrio* in the city, where the chilies were more expensive and tended to be over-dry. Phil headed in that direction.

He pulled up in front of Centro Pupusa y Alimentos Univer-sales and parked next to the store's delivery truck. He admired the name: universal foods. The newcomers had visions of grandeur, essential for immigrants from those poor places who after a generation or two would be living in houses bigger than his. His grandfather arrived with no skills, no money, no language, burdened by an antique religion that kept him on the margins of his new society and a traumatic past equal to these Latinos, and now his grandson was making a living, or at least had at one point, by returning to the country the old man had fled to save his skin. He owed him something. Actually, he owed him everything, starting with his life. How could he thank the dead man? The only way was through magazine stories. His name, according to some papers he had discovered, was Meyer Wolf. Phil didn't believe the name was real. An immigrant in those conditions couldn't be a wolf. And Meyer? Too German to be true.

He was dreaming those optimistic, liberal Western dreams when Dana walked into his field of vision. It took him a moment to realize that the girl in the strange get-up with a lot of skin showing was his daughter. She was lounging against the ice machine to the right of the front door of Centro Pupusa. The writing on the ice machine was in Spanish, and the girl was almost naked in red hot pants and a halter top and high heels, and an oversized pair of sunglasses with a fashion designer's logo glittering in the sunlight. Behind the lenses, she could be staring straight back at him.

He couldn't look, but he couldn't not look. Every man would have had the same dilemma, though not every man was her father. He forced himself. It was one of the hardest things he had done in his life as a parent. A hundred sacks of ice couldn't cool me down, her pose said. *I didn't know she had a sex.* Immediately he was ashamed of the thought. This wasn't sex, this was a parody of sex decked out in retro-fashion. Hot pants went out in the last century, and so did halter tops. Did she find that stuff at the Salvation Army? There was no outlet out here in the fields. She didn't need one. She surfed the net like everyone else. She didn't have to leave the house. But if she never went out the way he thought, how did she get here?

Phil steeled himself and stared at the exhibition again. Her tendons pulsed and bulged along the hem of her hot pants. The body's deep structure, anything but attractive, but he was not the intended audience. Then who was? What was his daughter saying? *Go ahead, feel free to study my anatomy, it is of no concern to me. I am outside it. I am the Visible Woman. See how my parts clash.* Dana's legs were slightly parted and tensed so that no one could miss her sinews against the red ice machine. There was one saving grace for Phil. No Latino, and those were the only men who shopped for groceries here except him, would get anywhere near a girl like that.

He recognized her strategy, and was sorry he did. He had fallen for it enough times when he was young, he finally learned to recognize it and make it part of his categories of predation. Messed up and proud. This was the age of pride in things you had no hand in creating. Black and proud, Jewish and proud, gay and proud. But here, pride was justified. Dana had created something, herself, she was a case of sui generis. Phil revised his thought about his daughter having no sex. There was no such thing as no sex, though there was sex he did not understand or appreciate. There were sexes, as many as there were people, and this was one of them, disorder as temptation. *I'm fucked up, so love me.* That was an irresistible offer. He had gone for girls with troubles just had they had chosen him, the unwritten contract again. He'd taken plenty of messed-up girls to bed a generation ago and here was karma returning to punish him for all the tears he had dried after he shot his wad, the brick of pain he traded for the feather of pleasure. The routine worked back then, and it must still work now. The lovemaking it generated was dreary, that was how he remembered it, what else could you expect from a girl when you claimed you were with her to help save her from herself? The contract cut both ways and hurt both sides, everyone pretending it didn't exist, and both sides using it to the hilt. He tried to unthink the thought of Dana being a partner in that sort of exchange, maybe with the guy she was sharing her anime drawings with. If she never went out, then where did it happen? But if she never went out, what was she doing here?

Then the scene exploded. It made perfect sense. Amy and Megan came out of the store. Amy never shopped here, and Dana never went out, and here they all were, the women in his life. There were any number of things he did not know about. Amy took Dana's hand and lifted her out of her slouching pose. They began to walk across the asphalt parking lot, Amy with Dana's hand in her hand and Megan on her other wing as reinforcement, security, though the look on Megan's face was resentful. Dana did not see that. Her face was illuminated, radiant in full sun, her exhibitionist's smile proud. Phil saw her so rarely in the upright position he had forgotten how tall she was compared to his wife, her elongated body thin, an El Greco figure in a strip mall parking lot. The three women walked slowly and deliberately toward him. The blacktop was a runway, and this a fashion show, a display of female flesh, mother and daughters, the elder with the physique of a camp survivor, though no one but Phil saw it that way, and her mother whose body had brought forth this creation, while the third did backup, pressed into the role and clearly wishing she were somewhere else, caught between having to protect her sister and needing to protect herself from her. Phil was afraid Dana's bones would snap under the pressure of their use. The women walked past his car and did not recognize it, and did not see him. They were not automotively oriented, they wouldn't have known the difference between a Swatch car and a Mercedes. Amy held fast to Dana's hand. The radiance on the girl's face was fixed as if it had been sprayed on with a contorting product like Botox. Who was the audience? On this dull, hot summer afternoon, the strip mall lot was empty but for him.

Megan kept one hand clamped on Dana's shoulder. He understood that she had moved into the basement to escape her older sister. It was a coping strategy. He knew that, sooner or later, the expiry date would come. No strategy works forever. Then Dana stumbled on a dip in the asphalt and Amy steadied her. You needed enormous inner strength for this kind of exercise. It took the women five minutes to reach the end of the parking lot. There was nowhere to go after that. The demonstration was over. They turned and retraced their steps past Phil's position, and then to Amy's car. What did *enabler* mean? You helped someone do something. You allowed them to do it. You made that person able. Did the word always carry negative freight, the way *complicit* did? Dana was radiant, she shone for an audience of herself, and Amy had the same proud light in her eyes, the transfer complete between the two women. It was Amy's revenge against him, her infidelity.

Then the three women got into her car and were gone. It made no logical sense, but he was sure Amy wanted him to see her, and understand how far ahead of him she was in the fight for their daughter's affection. He got out of his car and walked toward Centro Pupusa. On his way past the ice machine, he reached out and stroked its metal flank. It was warm to the touch, though inside it held ice.

In the store the clerks greeted him warmly but circumspectly. He was always the only gringo in the place, a convert to their culture whose real intentions were yet to be tested. A round-faced girl with a long braid was stocking the shelves by the dried chili bins. He asked her if a *gringa* had come in just now and bought *moritas*. She couldn't tell him. "I don't look at *gringas*," she confided, then moved off a little further, embarrassed to be talking to a man she didn't know.

He watched her do her job with exquisite concentration, her pink tongue pressing on the darker pink of her bottom lip. It was the kind of male look that had the store clerks wary and watching him. Some gringos, they knew, had a thing for Latina girls. Those guys thought their women were submissive. They didn't see the vigilance and distrust.

Phil picked up a *morita* and smelled its smoky heat and tried to understand what he had just seen. Amy did not like spicy food. At best, she tolerated his forays into Latino cooking. But she went to Centro Pupusa and took their daughters who were too old to go food shopping with their mother so that Dana could stay outside in the sun and exhibit her body against an ice machine. Once he had lamented to Amy that their daughter might never have a life as a woman the way she had had. The comparison was way off. Amy and Dana were in this display together, two women allied, a bond he could not equal, no matter how much time he spent in her room, reading her stories.

After the incident in the parking lot where Megan was wearing that resentful look, and with the message the Beauchard book sent, Phil went down to the basement to try and draw her out. He could read the look in her eyes. *You can't talk to her so you're settling for me, and besides, it's really none of your business.* After the initial rejection, which was just a way of testing his resolve, she began to talk. Her current boyfriend was named Tyler, but the way she described the relationship, there seemed to be two current boyfriends, though maybe both were named Tyler. Whether he was one or numerous, Tyler made strategic and liberal use of the basement exit. Megan did not think there was anything unusual about her parents not meeting the boy she was sleeping with. What was the point, they weren't sleeping with him, she was. It wasn't like she was going to marry him or anything. He was nice to her, he didn't make her do things she didn't want to, a lot of guys wanted oral or anal or both and weren't particularly drawn to the part that makes a woman a woman, guys like that were gay in her book, not that she had anything against gays.

She laid it all out for his benefit in a single sentence, without stopping for breath. Phil was relieved. His daughter had a clear moral code after all.

"I don't know if it's too much information," he told her. "But it is a lot."

"Well, you asked. You ought to know what it's like out there," she advised. "It's not all flowery fields of romance. Our love lives always end up in disaster."

"Then why do it?"

"How else am I going to find out anything?"

Megan had a point. She wasn't that different from the warriors of sexual liberation of his time who had laid down their bodies for the cause. With the ferocity of Red Guards, they sacrificed to destroy straight society's moral hypocrisy. They were brave, and paid for their bravery. Phil hoped Megan would find an attachment to someone once the adolescent horseplay was done, which might take a while. In his time it was called "experimenting." The word gave sleeping around an air of scientific inquiry, a program, a plan, which it was at times. Liberation was murder, especially on women. Phil knew a red-haired girl named Peggy who, to atone for slavery and slave traders to whom she claimed a distant family connection, slept with every black man who wanted her. She was proud of her sacrifice. It made her feel noble. He asked if her forebears had really owned or traded in slaves. "That's not the point!" she screamed. That was decades ago, but Phil could not avoid the picture of freckled Peggy and her pink flesh in the crucible of race warfare.

It could have been worse. What Megan was doing was the normal fare.

Then again, so was what Peggy had done, for her time.

"Your mother calls Tyler the Phantom."

"What does that mean? That he doesn't exist? That I don't really have a boyfriend? Thanks, Mom!"

"I think she'd like to meet him."

Megan shrugged. She wasn't going there.

"She saw him once on the way out."

"She told me. He's Asian."

"That's so absolutely not interesting anymore. Everyone's Asian. You know what he says? We're whiter than white."

"I think I'd like him."

"Yeah, well…"

"I won't get my hopes up." He turned to move upstairs. "I'm glad I talked to you. I feel better. I hope you do too."

"Okay."

That evening he related the conversation to Amy. Whenever

she found something offensive about Megan's moral behaviour, she blamed him because of the basement renovation. He didn't tell his wife not to worry, that their daughter had a solid moral code and a sense of herself as a woman and an object of desire. That would have meant repeating what Megan had said.

Once he had asked Amy what she told their daughters about the facts of life. She displayed the same discretion he did, and when he pushed her, she laughed at him.

"The facts of life? You mean the birds and the bees?"

It turned out she had only one message for her girls. *It's all about you. What you want.* Phil said nothing. That did not seem like advice a girl could live by.

Phil Brenner knew he was nowhere near the cutting edge of the day's sexualities. For him sex was a series of binaries, though he had been forced to grow more flexible recently, and not because of the raging in the media, including the outlets he wrote for, or used to. He looked back at his past life and saw he had been other things before settling into being a heterosexual. He did not consider that anything special. It was experimenting again, and that's what you did when you were young. But today, with such behaviour, he would have found himself in a category with the rules and variations that went with it. There were categories for every whim and hiccup of human choice, which limited the way people could think of themselves.

He knew there was something called asexuality, and another thing known as androgyny. They blurred together in his way of thinking, though he had enough knowledge of Greek roots to determine that they were not the same thing. Androgyny partook of both man and woman, and asexuality of neither. Though the latter could not exist. It was only an issue of denial.

The faces of Dana's anime drawings returned to question him after her performance in the parking lot. He had the usual Western face blindness: Asian features were unreadable to him. But there was more to it than that. Anime was a language of asexuality. Not androgyny, which is both, but neither—that was what he saw. The children in her drawings had nothing that determined them as being one sex or another. But their self-conscious, over-dramatic postures, even without a written story line, did not seem very childlike. They were pre-sex, though that state cannot exist either, Freud convinced everyone of that. The state, Phil concluded, was the denial of sex, a state that certainly exists, and one of the most common the mind is capable of producing. In her amateur art, without guile, Dana was drawing self-portraits, hundreds of them, or portraits of what she wanted to be, and sending them out into the world. The private had become hyper-public, which was intolerable, one more proof that he was dully conventional when it came to sexual practice.

Then what about the parking lot fashion show? It was parody. That could be a form of denial too. A kind of drag show, it occurred to him now, though at the time he was too shocked by the sight of his daughter's flesh to understand that. Did Amy realize her sex was being parodied by her daughter's mocking over-exposure? He was in no position to ask her. That was the problem with illicit knowledge, even when it is accidental. *I happened to be sitting in my car in a parking lot when you and our daughters happened to come strolling by and I saw something that chilled me...* He was sick of not knowing the things he wanted to know, and knowing only what he could not use. When it came to Dana though, he and Amy could swear solidarity with each other a thousand times, their daughter was a wedge between them.

71

Anime was a phenomenon of millions. It was not some specialized, exotic symptom Dana was producing on her own. A symptom always has a social value. Millions must have the same need she did. At the same time, society hypersexualized girls her age. Okay, he wanted to know, which one is it going to be?

The answer was both, and within the same person, many times over. That sounded like torture to him.

There was no imminent peril in seeking out Lynne, only curiosity, and though curiosity might have killed the cat, that happened only after its eighth life was used up, and Phil didn't figure he had spent any of his possible lives. A foolish thought for someone who had sought out risk for a living.

Lynne agreed to meet him at the Doll's House a second time. It was early enough in the evening for the waitress to be on duty. This time Phil avoided the Ibsen jokes. What turns a person into Captain Obvious? The need to be liked, no doubt, the harshest dictator the self can have.

Lynne was more playful, looser, if that was the right word, which made sense, since she had not just left a grief soirée, where loss filled half of every glass. Phil discovered she had the capacity for small talk, a relief to him. She worked as a history teacher, she told him, in one of the community colleges that served as a bridge to university for the timorous who needed encouragement to move up a notch, and the illusion of education for the rest. She taught world history, vast survey classes in amphitheaters lit like aquariums, often following the events of the day.

"Let me guess—Arabs."

"No, that's too specialized. They have someone for that—a real Arab. That's obligatory now. I do European. I'm Eurocentric.

With Putin in power, at least until further notice, I'm doing a lot of Russian."

"My daughter is interested in the Ukrainian famine."

"Ah. The *holodomor*, they called it. Stalin at his most typical. In nature, there is no such thing as famine. It is a human invention." Lynne squinted at him. "You're not Ukrainian, are you?"

"No."

"Just checking. Because that branch of history is completely ethnic, or almost. The only people writing it are Ukrainians, out to preserve the memory of Russian atrocity. So then...?"

"She got attached to the subject."

"I see. She chose it, or it chose her—can I put it that way?"

"You could."

Lynne shot first and apologized after. Her method was a relief after the tone of his discussions with Amy, with whom all conversation regarding Dana was circumspect and freighted with secondary and tertiary levels of blame. Lynne had the freshness of anecdote. She and Phil were telling stories to each other and trying to make them sound good, and thinking out loud in hopes of understanding something new in the presence of someone new. And they did not share the same pain, the way it was between Amy and him, and that produced a sense of lightness. This was seduction, the way it always is with a new story, even one that concerned loss. The erotics of loss exist after all.

"If they're good, all historians, even amateur ones, have a physical relation to their fields," Lynne told him.

"I never considered that."

"Come on, you must have the same connection to the stories you write."

"I suppose I do."

Lynne sniffed dismissively, as if she'd caught the stink of an outright and unsophisticated lie. "It's an attachment born of dis-order."

"That has occurred to me more than once."

"What part of the famine is your daughter interested in?"

"What people ate. You know, the boiled nettles and dandelions and grass. The stuff they ate to survive."

"It's amazing the things people will do to live until they finally give up."

"That's what she discovered."

"So she is your lost daughter."

"Yes," Phil allowed. It was all he could do to admit that, even to someone he had met at his grief counsellor's and with whom, on paper, he shared the defining events of his life. "The one who matches yours."

"Though different. Completely different. Loss may be what makes us human, the way our dear leader says, but no two losses can be the same."

"You're right. At least we're not estranged. I can go into her room and read her three-by-five cards about people eating nettles and dirt and sucking coal or whatever they did."

"Nettles are good for you. So is coal."

"May I never have to find out!"

Lynne smiled. When he was not being careful, Phil returned to the tone and cadence of someone who could have had roots in Dana's Ukrainian disaster. He was a candidate for one of those "Whose Story Are You Carrying?" workshops. Maybe a grief support group was not enough. Or maybe he was in the wrong group altogether. It might be worth his while to get acquainted with the mudmen and mudwomen who were his ancestors, and find out how and why they had come back to life inside his older daughter's mind at this particular historical and psychic moment. They were dybbuks, wandering, dissatisfied spirits, they had moved in, and now they were possessing Dana, and along with her they owned his wife and his other daughter and him too. That was one definition of disorder, antique but still vitally useful. There were wandering spirits out there with an urge to possess, like the dybbuks of the folktales and all their kin, and when they showed up to wreak havoc in the house, it turned out they were the self in different clothes, wearing the ancestors' rags. Why else would every group and band and tribe, every person, have that kind of folktale lodged in their hearts?

Lynne picked up her wine glass and stroked its stem, which unnerved him. Her daughter, she told him, would not return her calls or letters or e-mails, she spurned even the lowest form of communication, the text message. At one point Lynne received a summons from the director of the self-esteem community. It was the first personalized communication she received from the place, if you set aside the bills and dunning letters when she forgot to pay, and the appeals for donations, hardly personal, hardly communication. The director was a woman named Ilona Prakash, though most likely it was made up, a *nom de guerre*, a cover that let her do the dark and dangerous work of rebuilding girls' self-esteems. The first time she called Lynne, it wasn't to talk, but only to set up a further telephone appointment a few days later. Lynne recognized the strategy: make the parent wait, get her anxious and hyper-vigilant, soften her up the way artillery softens up enemy positions.

When the appointed time rolled around, Prakash did not disappoint. She ordered Lynne to cease and desist all attempts to communicate with her daughter. Her intrusions were counter-productive to the delicate process of reestablishing the girl's self-esteem.

75

"She actually said that to me!" Lynne yelled the words, and the barmaid with the nose ring glared across the room at them. "I pay the bills, don't I?"

"Is any of what happened supposed to be your fault?"

"I had a child. The child turned out to be a girl. That's my fault."

"I wonder whether your Ms. Prakash has children."

"I doubt it! Otherwise she would have shown more compassion."

Lynne looked at her wine glass and the smudged lipstick on its edge. *Lipstick traces.* That was supposed to be sexy, but its animal origins were clear in its greasy texture.

"You still think that if he pays for what he did, that won't help?"

Lynne raised her eyes from her glass. "Is this Dirty Harry, take two?"

"No. It's the investigative journalist in me."

"Don't waste your time. You don't have to investigate. I'll tell you everything. Where he lives, where he works. *I will show you the path of wisdom*—he teaches at a Catholic college. And he remarried and started a new family."

"With a daughter?"

"After two boys he got the girl he was going for."

"Goddamnit—you know he's going to reoffend! That's what they do. And we're going to let him?"

Phil was halfway out of his chair. She put her hand on his to keep him from dashing out the door.

"Every man wants to bring the abuser to justice. It's the way to my heart, they figure."

Phil settled back into his spot. The same was true for him. He would have given his heart completely to anyone who could have made Dana well.

"You haven't said your daughter's name."

"I can't. She won't let me."

When they stepped out of the Doll's House with its aggressive air conditioning, heat lightning was rolling along the horizon in shallow sheets of light. The parking lot light poles buzzed. In the orange glow, right out in front of everyone, had there been anyone, Phil held Lynne close by the front door of her car. She let him hold her, as long and as tightly as he wanted, but her arms did not lift from her sides. The embrace took place, though he could not say it was consensual. He felt the thrill of all the things he did not know about her and would never know, such as how long it had been since a man truly held her, and whether she still felt holdable at all, and how long it was since she took pleasure in this or any other part of the act. So much time fled without joy, that too was an unpunished crime, a waste of their time on earth, the weaknesses of the self standing between them and pleasure, even of the most modest kind.

A moment later, he pulled away.

"That makes me happy," Phil told her.

"Happier," she corrected him.

"Yes. As happy as my unhappiest."

"Sometimes I really hate those formulas. Dr. Sheridan and her treasure chest of sayings. So-called words to live by."

"I met you through her."

Lynne shrugged, noncommittal. "We think we're doing ourselves good. But we don't really know. Maybe it's the opposite."

"There must be a thousand societies that live quite well without grief counselling."

"No doubt. But we have it here, it is available… and I need help."

He took her in his arms again, carefully. He wondered what his embrace might feel like to her. He stepped away from the moment and saw himself as a stranger might. A *stranger* meant Amy, out on the kind of late-night errand she never ran, though she never went to the *pupusa* place either. A man and a woman holding each other—no, a man holding a woman—in the empty parking lot of a strip mall next to an automobile, under a light standard. What were the possible interpretations?

None, outside of endless sadness. Being sad with a woman who was not your wife could be seen as adultery. He smiled at that word—so conventional, so nineteenth-century.

"My daughter told me she might have a boyfriend."

"But I thought…"

"The Prakash woman told me. It was the one bone she threw."

"Then you should be happy."

"Why? He's not *my* boyfriend."

Before they had Dana, and then Megan, to the admiration and bewilderment of his colleagues and their wives who planned for children but could not take the leap, Phil agreed to Amy's dream of life lived in a house among the fields. Those were his days of wanting to please. "The space to grow," was her mantra. Children call out for space, Amy said, she could hear them calling even before they were born, and moving to the far-flung, open spaces was part of the contract completed with the arrival of the girls in what now seemed to him like quick succession. Quick, perhaps, but he did not regret it. Having the girls was among the few things he never regretted. In those days men would come to him as to a priest for advice. How do you do it, they asked. Be curious, he told them, the advocate of fertility triumphant. It is among the great human virtues. Tell me, do you like making love to your wife? He earned insulted looks for that question. Of course his friends liked it, though Phil had his doubts about their zeal. Then just let go. Look her in the eye and say *Yes*. Have your Molly Bloom moment, man-style.

He had been curious with Amy, he wanted to know what she could produce, he loved the way she looked and felt when she was pregnant, so big and almost masculine in her power. He did not imagine, when he moved out to the fields, that later he would suffer from the demoralizing emptiness of the landscape and the absurd layout of the streets. It was an arduous drive to his friend Bruno's place even when it was not rush hour. When the low factories of Silicon Valley without the valley gave way to something marked with the older stories of the industrial age, he felt more at home. Someone had lived here once, and left traces, and he liked that. These were the remains of the towns that had served the railroads and the farmers, and slowly they had been swallowed up by people's need to move further away from each other as the city grew out in all directions.

Phil had read about a phenomenon called the teardown. It was a zoning issue that had been solved by permits, which was another way of saying *money*. People bought houses not to live in them, and renovate them to suit their new self-image, but to tear them down entirely and root out the foundations and build something better on the lot. Better meant bigger, right to the allowable edges of the property line, with no space wasted for backyards where laundry might flap in the wind on a clothesline, or an apple tree might grow. The act repudiated the previous owners who were dumb enough to have accepted life in a smaller house. But they might be excused. They came from a humbler century that had not discovered the glories of debt.

Arriving at Bruno's, he put his gift bottle on the kitchen table. "Just this one. I swear."

Bruno ignored his self-promise.

"Tell me some news."

Phil obliged by venturing into a painful and partial relation of his last evening with Lynne.

"If you don't want her," Bruno said, "perhaps I would like her. I would not hurt her feelings the way you have. I would not take the first step, then stop."

Bruno's portrait was crude but it made sense. People wanted to be desired, and desire's sting did not lessen with age, at least not for everyone. Bruno was Phil's friend, and Phil paid dearly for the friendship with his wife's sarcastic appraisals, so he might as well confide in him. Otherwise, there was no friendship, and no point in being here.

"I didn't not want her. I put my arms around her."

"You consoled her."

Bruno made it sound like Phil had slapped her in the face.

"The situation is delicate," Phil explained.

"I have lived through several delicate situations in my life. The only way out is to keep living. Eventually something changes."

Phil considered the mess of Bruno's apartment. The place was an exercise in self-punishment. It was also a commitment to a way of living without attachments. Phil did not want that. He wanted greater bonds, not fewer.

"You and your lady friend are united by your daughters. But they stand between you like guardrails."

Bruno turned to a line of framed coloured drawings that sat on an ornate wooden buffet with baroque heaviness. "Look at the beautiful pictures my daughter made. She was young—

nine, ten years old. She did not even know what she was doing. I was afraid to tell her how good she was. I was afraid she might stop."

"And she did," Phil deduced.

"She became committed to alcohol."

"So that is your loss."

Bruno shrugged off the word. "It is a loss for art, and for her."

They stared at their wine glasses and wondered about their own commitments. These were not wine glasses, but orange juice tumblers made to hold wine. The lack of stemware was part of Bruno's general sacrifice. Add that to the roiling cat-litter box and the disdainful Abyssinian that glared at Phil, the newcomer, the intruder. The décor was refreshing. Phil felt comfortable in Bruno's disorder, a place of a man without a woman. Bruno was free to express himself without restraint.

"You are very fond of this word *loss*. It has developed some fetishistic value for you."

"I don't know about that. A fetish is supposed to bring pleasure."

"Come now, fetish is not pleasure, it is pathology!" Bruno glanced at the pictures that he must have spent endless evenings contemplating. "I am not happy about my daughter preferring alcohol to art. Maybe I should blame myself. I have provided a bad example. Okay, but I blame this place too. There is no incentive or encouragement to work, only to party. Parties I can understand, when there is brotherhood, for an evening. But here they are something sinister that makes you isolated."

Phil looked at the drawings. They were good, more than good, too good, unnaturally better than anything a ten-year-old girl should be able to produce, the tragedy of the wunderkind. Maybe that was the problem: she was a prodigy who got bored.

Behind the drawings stood a collection of dolls, fabric, and coloured paper attached to schematic human forms that had been coaxed out of small, stubby glass milk bottles. This girl had had her golden age. Then she quit. He recognized the pattern. Dana had excelled in one pursuit after another when she was a girl, track and field, flute, karate, he didn't know what became of all the medals and ribbons she had won. She stepped onto the top step of the podium, received her reward, then walked off the stage for good. Was that boredom, he wondered, or the understanding that she didn't need to prove anything to anyone anymore. She quit because she had never enjoyed the things she was so good at.

"It doesn't look like my daughter is halting her research, unfortunately. She's sticking to it like glue."

"Yes. You told me. It's strange, but don't say *unfortunately*. Clearly she's atoning for past crimes she could not have possibly committed. Maybe you committed them."

"Yes. I committed the Ukrainian famine. I ordered it."

Bruno raised his glass. "You were the one who sent in the locusts to eat the wheat."

"There were no locusts. There were Soviets."

"Same thing. When in doubt, blame the Russians!"

"She is suffering from systemic guilt."

"Systemic. I've heard that word before. Remind me what it means."

He smelled another Bruno joke, since no one could be unaware of everything that word stood for. Phil kept waiting for *systemic* to disappear, but it showed no signs of going anywhere. Instead, it was devouring the landscape. It meant you were guilty of oppression or abuse or worse, whether you committed those acts or not, because you belonged to a certain segment of a certain society that practiced oppression and abuse and worse. Systemic was dynamic and as ever-changing as disorder itself, it changed position depending on the fate and fashion of your particular cohort, and the cohorts you were not part of. You could have been a member of an oppressed minority when you were growing up, and an outrageous oppressor later on in adult life, without ever having done anything personal. *Systemic* was like disorder itself, restless, looking for new attachments, a dybbuk. Phil was gigantically hostile to it because it took away all individual responsibility. It made people reckless. If you were an oppressor or a racist or a rapist or someone who engaged in non-consensual sex with his wife, but only systemically, you might as well go ahead and do those things in real life since you were going to get charged with them anyway.

Of course he did not do those things. Uselessly, he clung to his moral high ground. And he knew better than to engage systemic in debate. He could not possibly win, unless earning new enemies was considered victory. The only person he shared his ad absurdum arguments with was Bruno, who feasted on them with cynical delight. It was not a happy situation.

"You can make fun of systemic, and I might agree with you," he warned Phil, "but it is ruining your life. More to the point, your daughter's life. With all this guilt about the Ukrainians, she is a victim of it."

"Madness is using systemic. Excuse me, not madness. Disorder."

"And if systemic did not exist, it would use something else, is that it?"

"Yes. It would. It would find another attachment. It is forever wandering."

"But then its form would be different. So it would actually *be* different, in reality. You would have a different daughter. You would be a different man."

83

They argued back and forth for hours, fed by wine and the pleasure of feeling excluded by the society of systemic, which made them superior beings in their own minds. Wine had that same effect. Why do I drink so much with Bruno, Phil wondered. By the time he left his place, the smell of Abyssinian feces had burrowed deep into his clothes. Outside, the humidity increased its intensity, since Bruno kept his apartment frigidly air-conditioned, the sign, for him, that he had successfully mastered the ways of the American continent. The only antidote to cat litter was a long walk to air out his shirt. His sweat would replace cat stink. At least it would be a human smell, and the walk would give Phil's pores the chance to open up and expel a measure of red wine. An evening with Bruno, Amy told him each time, was nothing more than a permission to drink to excess.

The house where he grew up was a mile or so from Bruno's place, a twenty-minute walk on a warm night. How that house came to be built, how and where it stood, was the stuff of family legend, full of contradictory and possibly untrue stories. A Dutch contractor named Jakob Boeder built it at cost, apparently because Phil's father had been part of a loose committee of people sponsoring refugees after the war from countries that had been overrun by the Nazis. The building was Boeder the carpenter's thank-you note. Phil did not know whether everyone on the committee received a house at cost. That would have added up to a lot of work. Boeder began by buying a lot at the end of a street that dead-ended against a freight yard that had since been converted into condos. This, the Dutchman explained to Phil's father, was the only way to beat the restrictive covenant. Boeder was a fast learner. Most native-born people did not know what that illegal but common practice was about.

Real estate agents banded together and refused to sell lots and houses to certain types of people unwanted by the neighbours on a particular street. With his accent and gaunt appearance, Boeder was odd, but he corresponded to nothing people wanted to keep out. Dutch courage, Dutch treat, double Dutch—the Dutch had been figures of fun at one point, but that mockery had faded long ago. They had been Allies in the war.

Boeder built a small square box and clothed it in green wood shingles. The master bedroom was no bigger than the others in keeping with his Communist ideals. The house had no porch, front or back, the floors were asphalt tiles with linoleum in the kitchen, and the roof was shingled too. The number of windows that could be opened were kept at a minimum. Maybe the model for the house could be found in Holland, where cool breezes blew in from the North Sea, but not in this country with its hot, humid summers. No porch meant no contact with the neighbours, which was a good idea, since they hated this family who had cheated the restrictive covenant by going through Boeder to buy the lot. Whether this design was Boeder keeping the budget low, or his comment on the neighbours whom he had tricked, no one could say.

As Phil walked toward it in the sticky night air, he understood that his boyhood and his family's life were casualties of Jake Boeder's house. It was a doll's house, a miniature, something a boy might make with plastic blocks that came in a play set. There was no house like it on the street, so stripped of decoration, so bare, no porch to sit on and drink a beer and gossip with the neighbours, a Puritan house, a Calvinist dwelling inside and out. Phil and his brothers were not allowed to use the front door during the winter. It opened directly onto the living room with no transition, and the cold wind blew unchecked into the room. The family lived under the thumb of Boeder's design, and his outsmarting the covenant, that act of trickery the neighbours never forgave. The house was a scale model of the Dutchman's mind.

He remembered two things. Boeder had died in a mental institution, which everyone attributed to his wartime experiences. It made sense that his houses oppressed the people who tried to live in them. His at-cost gift turned out to be poison. And that once during a fight with one of his brothers, Phil had slammed his fist through the windowpane.

He had not thought about that incident in decades. He was a little boy with a sunny disposition who liked pleasing adults, then one day he exploded. The most surprised member of the family, after him, was his mother. She had taught him the art of laying low and letting the shit fly past overhead. His outburst was a betrayal of her education, and the unspoken treaty between them: *this is how we handle our place in the family*. Suddenly the other people who lived in the house—he did not spontaneously use the word *family* any more than he would say *home* for *house*—turned wary of him. They began keeping a respectful distance. It was magic: put your small boy's fist through a pane of glass and you got respect. It also earned him punishment. His father ordered him to buy a new piece of glass and glaze the window. That meant going to the hardware, having the glass measured and cut, buying putty and a putty knife since his father did not have a single tool in the house and was proud of that fact. The punishment involved money too. Phil had to pay for everything. But his father's plan backfired. Phil enjoyed going to the hardware and associating with the men who worked there in their blue-shirted uniforms. For once he felt normal, doing normal physical work like everybody else, a competent person with concrete abilities, not to mention the badge of a bandaged hand.

He stopped under a streetlight and examined his hand. The scar still lay across his knuckles. He had lost touch with the impulses that came from having a bad temper. That was part of the slump too.

Stroking the decades-old scar, he managed to walk right past his house. Where his house had been. He stood and considered what stood in its place. It was as he expected: his house had been torn down. There was no time in his childhood that he looked back on with longing, that supposed age of innocence with all its nostalgia. He was not offended that Jake Boeder's house had been demolished, foundation and all, and replaced with a fantasy that rose up above a double garage that dominated its front. Phil recognized the problem and sympathized with the man who had ordered the place built. There was no room on the lot for a garage, not if you wanted a house like this. Incorporating the garage into the building, making it the centrepiece, what came at you when you looked on it from street level, advertised his level of debt, and the fearless lifestyle that demanded. No doubt there was an suv and a boat behind the closed garage door, protected by the glare of an outdoor lighting system. Phil was much too timid to take on debt of that level. Fast times had arrived on Jake Boeder's lot, all 50 by 150 feet of it. The house rose two storeys above and behind the garage. The owners could keep watch on the street from their porch on the garage's flat roof, next to the massive barbecue and gas torches and acacia deck furniture. The design was ingenious. They could sit outside, but still be above their neighbours. In typical teardown style, there was no room wasted on a yard or a driveway.

You can't go home again. That was a dreary cliché, since no healthy adult would want to go back to the past. He had suffered from living in that house, and so had his brothers and parents, though they never spoke about it, either then or now. These days, where they resided, his parents were as unlikely as ever to talk about their feelings. The only way to get them to do that would be to turn them into characters and make them speak, and he was not in the fiction business. His brothers were still on this earth, aliens to him, actively keeping to themselves. There was nowhere to go for shared memories. Phil looked up at the towering monument. He had been unhappy in the house that once stood here, but he felt no pleasure at seeing Boeder's heartfelt gift replaced by this bulging monstrosity that fit onto the modest lot the way a fat man's belly fits into his shirt.

"What are you looking at? I'm calling the cops."

That was inevitable. The owner was standing at the railing of his porch one story up with a drink in his hand. Phil made a quick and hopefully accurate calculation. If the guy was threatening to call the police, he probably wouldn't shoot him. His position was dominant, a whole floor above Phil. He didn't think *Stand your ground* would apply here.

"I used to live here. I mean, in the house that was here before yours."

"You're bullshitting me!"

Phil heard alcohol talking. "No, for real."

The man drew himself up. "That was the most miserable excuse for a house I've ever seen."

"You don't know the half of it."

"How the hell did anyone ever live in it?"

"It took real skill. You had to know how to fold yourself up into a little package to fit inside, like a Chinese contortionist.

And you had to be fast to make it to the door and escape. It was training for life. That's why I'm in such great shape now."

Phil could see the man thinking from his dominant position on the garage roof. First, his displeasure at not getting a rise out of a stranger he figured he had successfully insulted, and then the prospect, vague at first but quickly developing, that this passer-by with a tenuous connection to him might be his drinking buddy for what remained of the night.

"You've got a lot more room now," Phil congratulated him.

"I'm living large."

"I hope you're not all by yourself up there."

"Fuck you! I mean, really, fuck you."

Phil saw the man cock his hand to throw his glass, then saw his change of heart when he realized there was still a drink in it. The confrontation was as inevitable as Oedipus and the stranger where three roads met, the apparently senseless altercation orchestrated by the gods. But there was good reason for this one: a hot night, a string of drinks, the old and the new, the original and the interloper, if you believed in originals, the humble settler and the nouveau riche.

"I'm going to melt away into the night where I came from, now that I've delivered my message."

"You don't have any fucking message."

"Sleep it off, big boy!"

Phil was relieved to get out of the glare of the house lights, and into the protective darkness. He would have fought the man as Oedipus had fought the stranger, he would have done everything in his power to kill him, though he was armed with nothing but bad memories of the house that no longer occupied the lot. No, not bad memories. Just memories. One story of vertical elevation kept the confrontation from breaking out. And the fact that the gods had pulled back, and were no longer making sport with mortals.

Amy sniffed showily when Phil came into the master bedroom.

"It could be worse. I should thank my lucky stars. It could be some other woman's perfume."

"What do I smell like?"

"Cat shit. Plus the usual manly tavern essence."

"Sounds attractive."

"Let's just say I'm used to it."

As he stripped off his stinky clothes, stinky to Amy's nose but not his, he told her the story of the fight that had not taken place, of Oedipus and Laius, how two total strangers could fly into a murderous rage, one against the other. As he talked, he understood that he and the man on the rooftop porch were anything but strangers. They were intimately bound by a narrow 50-by-150-foot lot. The man saw in Phil exactly what he was: a living reproach, a critique of his ostentatious lifestyle. Phil was the house he had ordered torn down and replaced with a monument to his ascension into fantastic heights of debt. Phil had a right to rail against the way Jake Boeder's house cramped his family's life. But it was his house. He would not let some arrogant stranger mock it, then tear it down. Phil needed that house, if only to hate it, the way everyone needs their enemies in order to discover who they are.

Phil got into bed and eased over toward his wife's side.

"I want to be reassured without necessarily having to do anything," she told him.

That certainly beat *Not tonight, honey, I have a headache.* His wife was ingenious, a true poet of rejection. That was a genre in itself.

He retreated to his side of the bed. The people who tell you not to write about them—those are the ones you have to write about. They're urging you into the act. It's a dare.

Tomorrow, he promised himself. The slump ends tomorrow.

Phil knew he was exposing himself to intrigue, not to mention cliché. Falling in love with the material was a running gag among long-form journalists and think-piece writers. They called the dangerous and common practice *marrying the subject*, and he had married a few already. With Bruno calling his visit a pre-confession, he could not miss the suggestion that soon he would cross the line that separates a journalist from his material. He could not picture how that might happen with Lynne—it was too unlikely. He had lost the ability to imagine, and that in itself was part of the slump. If it kept on, pretty soon he wouldn't be able to stand himself.

"So soon?" Lynne asked over the phone. "Didn't we just see each other?"

"Am I coming on too strong?"

Lynne didn't answer. Phil told her what he wanted. She gave him her ex-husband's address.

"Leave your Magnum at home, Dirty Harry."

"Rest assured, I don't have one."

"My daughter has lost so much. She doesn't need to lose her father."

The piece about hushing up and divulging taught him how and why that worked. Girls defended their abusers. Defending the abuser was part of denial, and just the beginning of greater injustices.

Phil was glad he had thought to bring some reading material to keep him company as he sat in front of the Godbold house in his car. *Nomen est omen.* The name fit a man who was an unpunished child abuser—a rapist, call the act what it was.

He wondered if Lynne's daughter kept the last name, or if she had any choice? *Godbold* did not suit a girl who lived in a community dedicated to rebuilding her self-esteem, and being cut off from everything that might interfere with the work. That name would go on mocking her forever. Imagine carrying the name of a man who had done those things to you.

He picked up a sheaf of dog-eared papers from the passenger seat. Every half page or so, he looked up to make sure he was not missing anything significant. The paper was recycled. On the back side was a legal document describing the tenets of a class action suit journalists had initiated against a media giant that sold their electronic rights without permission or payment. The writers had won a Pyrrhic victory. Just before losing the suit, the chain neatly slipped into protective bankruptcy and never paid a penny.

"Coefficient of Supportive Behaviors in Abuse Communities." He chose the article out of the thousands on the subject available online, printed it out and stowed the papers in his bag, away from Amy. All the time he was working on it, she considered the hush-to-divulge piece prurient and distasteful, and compromising to her situation as a communications officer at the hospital. He did not want to have that conversation again, this time without the benefit of paid employment. The article stayed out of sight.

"Abuse Communities"—it sounded like a contradiction, but no more flagrant than the community he belonged to, and willingly so. He stopped arguing with the title and read on.

Every piece he read might be that open door he was looking for, the way into an impossible subject, even the articles with doubtful titles, though that was a lot to ask from a random text pulled off the Internet, his navigation history erased once he was finished. But somewhere his traces were preserved. His commitment was noted should anyone care to investigate.

The subject was vital, but the writing was as dry as old putty, and loaded with statistics and mathematical formulas. The author didn't *believe* what she was saying; she was *suggesting*. Wow, the courage of your convictions, he addressed her. A subject made of blood and fear, and she reduced it to sawdust. Trauma was lessened, she asserted—no, she suggested—and resilience increased if the abuse victim spoke to a supportive person. Everybody knew that. Just the way everyone knew that if the supportive person turned out to be rotten, which often happened, the effect was reversed.

One type of bad listener was the worst, and that was the kind who hijacked the abuse victim's experience and made it her own. The author labelled this type "the egocentric."

There were people who liked to suck the experience out of other people's lives. In the absence of that thing called "a life," they downloaded their thrills from other people. The Latinos from the pupusa joint had a word for that, he overheard it once and worried they were talking about him. *Chopacolores*, colour-suckers. A person who did that could damage the people he was stealing from, though Phil would have to think about how that worked. Were experience thieves egocentric? He didn't see it that way.

Naturally, he tried the charge on himself. Would his interest in Lynne increase her trauma and lessen her resilience? Were all journalists *chopacolores* by nature?

He put the article back on the passenger seat.

Phil had come to this address in search of the unwritten contract that bound Lynne and her daughter and her ex-husband together, and enabled what had happened. He assumed there was one. If he sat here long enough, and was observant enough, he might catch sight of it, and even read it if he was lucky. He had no genius for breaking into houses. He would have to start here, on the outside.

He had watched any number of cop shows on TV and the big screen, and many of them featured surveillance sequences, the hero cop and his partner bored out of their minds, sitting in an unmarked car, drinking sour coffee out of Styrofoam cups and making threatening noises about whomever they were watching. Hardly Phil's case. He had no case, and what he was watching for was invisible. An excellent start, he decided.

As he waited, he thought about the conventions of those TV shows. When there was a sex scene, and there was always one, but usually no more than one, it was there to move the plot forward. The hero beds the babe, and intimacy leads to information, revelation, deep trouble, death threats—the plot is hurtled forward toward the end. That was the problem with marital sex, and why it was so rarely shown on TV. Marital sex does not move the plot forward. At best, it may be a tender affirmation or a surprising rediscovery, more often it consists of going through the motions, but it is never a plot point. That was why sex scenes on the screen were always so stilted. They were not about sex at all. They were about moving the story forward.

He thought back to the scene he had witnessed in the parking lot of Centro Pupusa. His jealousy leaped up at how Amy had outdone him when it came to their daughter, how deep her engagement was with Dana as two women in league with each other.

Then the surface jealousy fell away like a flimsy sheet, and he saw the real picture. It was startling. It was Amy putting her body on display in the parking lot, trying on the stance of a new woman, with their daughter as a prop for her experiment. That same body, she had told him in bed a few nights earlier, that she couldn't imagine using to make love with. The revealing hot pants and halter top slipped onto Amy's body, the ice machine and the oily blacktop setting her off like a jewel in a ring, a thousand times more alluring than the skinny uncertain girl she was walking next to.

Then a feature of the Godbold house stole his attention. He looked and looked at the quiet suburban façade. It was the ivy. The way it covered the bricks. The ivy had been allowed, or trained, to grow over the upstairs windows. It formed a permanent exterior curtain. Phil wondered about the light in those rooms, the dim atmosphere, the outside world filtered away. He had heard somewhere that ivy wasn't good for brick façades because it caused cracks to form in the mortar. The advantage of having a full-time curtain must have been greater than the damage done to the brickwork.

It's just fucking ivy, Phil reminded himself.

But it concealed something. He was sure of it. He pictured a piece of furniture in an upstairs room, a desk with a single drawer. And in the drawer, at the very back, a document. It was a contract, unwritten and unsigned and possibly unspoken, but a contract all the same. It stood behind the exchanges made and the permissions taken.

Then Phil imagined himself easing out of the car and slipping over the front lawn of the house and through the gap under the door. He had become a vapour, a foreign agent, a ghost. His slump was getting to him. It was making him desperate for discovery. He moved up the stairs into the room with the ivy growing over the window. It is no effort to get into a desk drawer when you're a wisp of transparent fog working on a hunch and an instinct for what is hidden. He went straight for it, and it was there as he thought it would be, at the back of the drawer. But it was not what he was expecting. The contract did not cover the new wife and the new daughter. It was the original one Godbold had used with Lynne, drawn up for their marriage, but apparently still powerful because it had been cut-and-pasted for the second marriage.

When he read it, his heart went out to Lynne. Godbold had clothed his intentions in the language of liberation, but with labyrinthine turns of phrase that pointed to everything he was hiding. A wife would have to be well versed in hermeneutics to see what he was getting at. He granted himself the poet's sovereignty over the others who lived under his roof. This was not marriage. It was a cult. He had dominion over those around him in the name of experience, a new god that abolished the need for permission. The perverted plagiarist, he had even stolen a line from Blake about childhood inhibition and purity and the adult world that sought to exploit it, then turned it on its head: *songs of experience.*

Phil was shocked, as shocked as he had been the night Lynne told him about the abuse. He couldn't blame her. She had been a young wife with a charismatic husband. She could not have anticipated where this would lead. Her guilt must be overpowering. He understood that, and felt something like love for her, but a love closer to pity and sadness. And the contract produced two little girls unequipped to fight back when the time came. There was a blank spot in the place where *No* went. They never learned to say the word. *If someone tells you not to tell, the first thing you do is tell.* He had said that to his daughters when they were young, probably too young. They stared at him and nodded. They didn't know what he was talking about.

The man who drew up the contract taught college. The intellect was a tool of corruption. Lynne's joke about Dirty Harry was no joke. If Phil had had a gun in the glove compartment he would have taken it out and aimed at the front door with cool resolve. A crime had been committed. Righting the wrong sounded virtuous. Many murderers have felt the same. The difference was that Phil had no gun.

He slipped out of the house and back across the cool grass to his car. The front door of the Godbold house opened and a girl ran across the lawn. She was wearing a dress with flowers on it. She sprinted toward the family car, an suv of course. The mother and two teenage boys followed. Phil watched the girl. She looked like an absolutely ordinary ten-year-old.

Everyone got into the vehicle. The kids in back, the mother in front, in the passenger's seat. Were they just going to sit there?

A minute later, Godbold came out of the house. He was tall and thin and greying and conventionally handsome and wore a blue sports coat in the warm air. He reached back to arm the security system, locked the door, then pulled twice on the doorknob. Compared to the rest of the family, it took him an hour to move from the front door to the driver's seat.

He got in behind the wheel and the car swept past Phil's position. Nothing visible had happened, but the accomplishment was enormous. He had read the contract and his heart opened to Lynne.

As he drove to the Doll's House to meet Lynne afterward, he looked for and did not find a way to tell her those things. There were no words yet for his feeling inspired by pity for the situation she had been in and forgiveness—not him forgiving her, but the forgiveness he wanted her to have for herself. He was afraid of being misunderstood. Lynne had the will to mis-understand him. He couldn't blame her. He was a man.

She was at a table in a far corner. She stood up when he came in.

"Did you see any monsters?"

"Yes, one. But it took a while. I almost fell asleep. I'm tired these days. Beyond tired."

"Maybe you have some kind of syndrome."

The charm of the Doll's House was wearing thin for him. It was time to find another venue without a snarky, nose-ringed barmaid and an absent-minded waitress who made a show of not noticing them. Phil wondered how the place made a go of it. Maybe other kinds of commerce were conducted on the premises.

"The house has ivy growing on it."

"Meaning?"

"Nothing, really. He pulls on the door twice after he locks it, once he's set the alarm system."

"He's a security-conscious guy. I didn't see it at the time."

Lynne took a long, unhappy pull from her wine.

"I'm paying for my girlish foolishness. It's not fair. I wasn't worse than anyone else. I did a lot fewer crazy things than most women. He'd published a slender volume of verse, and I thought that was cool. Marrying a poet! And he had those Waspy patrician manners. He had money, or so I thought. I used to like those dresses from *Vogue*."

"You were a social climber."

"You make it sound so elegant. Jesus Christ, why am I here? If I wanted insults I could look in the mirror."

"Sorry. Marriage is always about that. Getting more solid in life. Moving up."

They stared into their glasses. Phil's was white, straw-coloured, and Lynne's black-red, opaque, with no glints of light.

"I would picture myself in bed with him, a wife, his wife. I would look across the room and see the pretty dresses hanging on the back of the chair, so sexy, even without me in them. The dress I just took off, or that he took off me."

"That's a beautiful picture."

"It was the lead-up to disaster."

"But you couldn't have known that, could you?"

"The woman I was back then couldn't. But I was getting plenty of flack. That was the problem. When you get attacked, you defend, and you don't always get the point of the attack. Right after we were married, his little sister took me out for drinks. I thought it was going to be one of those welcome-to-the-family occasions. Hardly. She started right in on me. He didn't have his own money, it all belonged to his family, I'd gone for the prize and gotten caught in the trap. A leg-hold trap—she was one of those puritan types, animal rights, vegetarian before it got fashionable. She said the only way to free myself was to gnaw my leg off."

"Very considerate. Whatever happened to *Sisterhood is powerful*?"

"There's no such thing. After everything happened with my daughter, she tracked me down. She sat me down and told me he'd abused her when she was a girl, and that was why she was so short. She stopped growing after it happened."

"Why didn't she tell you before?"

"It happened to her, so it might as well happen to my daughter. That was her reasoning. The more damage, the better."

Viscerally, in his flesh, Phil still did not comprehend. Part of him could not believe that things like that happened, though he understood how closed systems work, he had written about it enough. Everyone kept the silence. It was like being in a religious order. The holy order of abuse. The original contract was not in the desk drawer behind the curtain of ivy. It lay in Godbold's parents' house, or grandparents', it was generations old.

"That was her revenge. She wanted me to know the guy I was sleeping with had been with her first. But mostly, it was political. Men are garbage, and here's more proof. Is that the basis for sisterhood?"

"Nobody else said anything?" In his pain for her, his outrage, Phil grasped for a solution that was not there. "The boyfriend who told you not to marry him?"

"He didn't treasure me. He was careless."

"Didn't your parents help?"

"'You stink, Lynne.'"

"Pardon me?"

"That's what my mother would tell me when I came home from being with a boy. She'd sniff the air and wrinkle up her nose. She didn't appreciate my curiosity."

Curiosity and carelessness, that had been the age. He had been careless too, and maybe still was. He certainly was trying. Lynne toyed with the stem of her glass.

"I saw that guy a while back. The one who told me not to marry my husband. He came out of nowhere."

"Where's nowhere?"

"The seventies. The woodwork. He's a seventies leftover. He wants me back. Can you imagine?"

"You could take him back."

"How free do you think my heart is? You said you were tired, more than tired? Imagine me."

Phil ordered two more glasses of wine from the disapproving waitress. There was something about the job she clearly did not understand, scowling at her customers when they ordered more drinks.

It's because we're too old for this. Wooing belongs to the young. If only she knew how it dies, but never dies.

When they had finished, after the second glass, he stood in the parking lot and watched Lynne drive away. Her heart was not free. Well, whose was?

When Phil Brenner was unlucky enough to remember a dream, it would settle on him like a succubus and return dawn after dawn. What was the use of the repetition—did it think he hadn't gotten its point the first time? The dream would become so dreary he grew bored with it, no matter how startling and strange its imagery had been the first time.

It ran like this. Its point of departure lay long in the past, a visit to the Guanajuato mummy museum in Mexico, for once not part of an assignment. In the museum, naked women and men were laid out in glass display cases. Many of the women still had wisps of maidenhair, and he could not keep his eyes off their vaginas and the double invitation there: I may be dead, but that shouldn't stop you from loving me. As people wandered unconcerned past him, reading the philosophical musings about death that accompanied the dried figures, he gazed and imagined them as sexually vibrant women sharing his bed, his life. Their bodies were as dry and friable as desert earth, and their faces contorted by time and the effort they needed to die. Then desire marched onto death's territory. Lynne was nowhere in the dream, but she was at its heart. Somehow, he felt in the dream, he had been to bed with her, he had made love to her and did not understand that until now. As he was wrestling with that illogical turn, the dream's focus switched. The last thing he saw before waking was Iris Chang in a glass display case. Over her breasts lay the book that had brought her fame, then disaster. The book was fresh and new, in mint condition, opened just once. She was dressed in a cap and gown and mortarboard.

Iris Chang was Dana's doing. Just as he was getting used to anime comics, Dana changed directions. Phil had never heard of Iris Chang until his daughter's restless investigations turned her way. The day he came across the name in Dana's wanderings, he went to the university library; he was an excellent pupil. He had no formal affiliation, but his status as an independent scholar, a lovely and outmoded classification, gave him the right to check out books. Iris Chang was a Chinese-American historian who had written about the Rape of Nanking by the Japanese, an atrocity overshadowed by the war that followed, but no longer in the shadows thanks to her account. Phil checked out the book, then sat in the library and read it in one sitting. He dropped it into his bag, where it would keep company with the abuse communities study.

Why was Dana shifting to China? He thought of the name, the Rape of Nanking, and felt heartsick.

Then he did what everyone does. He went online. Iris Chang had killed herself. At the height of her fame, after going on TV talk shows, with a bestselling book, the academic's dream and his too, she shot herself in her car with a decorative antique pistol, the kind Japanese officers carried when they raped Nanking.

That evening he knocked on Dana's door.

"Now what?" she called.

Phil cut to the chase.

"Are you thinking of doing yourself harm?"

She looked at him as if he were speaking a foreign language.

"Do you have suicidal thoughts?"

"Where does that come from?"

He told her what he had learned about Iris Chang. She laughed.

"You're so obvious! You're so superficial! You don't even know how the Internet works."

Because he had not found it, though it was everywhere online, she told him about the cult devoted to Iris Chang. The Chang family romance, she called it, which included Iris' mother and a crowd of virtual mourners who kept the conspiracy, or tragedy, depending on how you looked at it, alive, as they would the cult to a saint. The followers were everywhere if a person knew how to look.

"I looked."

"You didn't. You panicked. You didn't go past Wikipedia. You didn't turn the pages."

"Okay, okay. I was concerned. Is that all right?"

Dana shrugged. "I don't know."

She told him the first part of the story, which he knew, but not in the depth she possessed. The almost otherworldly success of a timid Asian woman academic who discovers material about a forgotten massacre and, using the word *rape* in the title, writes a book about the event. It was solidly researched and accessibly written, there were many books with the same qualities, but Iris' work—Dana was on first-name basis with the dead woman—stood out because of her identification with the subject. Iris felt the massacre in her flesh, and she made you feel it too, through her shyness, her demureness, her gift for suffering. The pornography of violence helped too. People were willing to read graphic descriptions of sexual atrocity with a clear conscience because they were contained in an academic book. Iris was their enabler.

At the height of her fame, she shot herself in the head.

Dana lay on her bed in her baggy work clothes. Phil tried very hard not to think about her and suicide.

"So far, I get it," he told Dana.

"Plenty of people don't think it was suicide. They think she was murdered. The Japanese killed her for giving them a bad name. You know how image-conscious they are. Saving face and all that."

Saint Iris. She would have never killed herself. She was at the height of her powers. She had displayed no symptoms. There was no apparent cry for help. A person doesn't kill herself out of the blue. She was a striver, an overachiever, and she succeeded with a bestselling book. This was not the profile of a suicide. The Japanese were happy to have her dead, and to frame the act as self-death. It discredited her thesis.

"Writing history is dangerous," Dana told him, "when you get involved physically. But that's how you reach genius. And death, sometimes."

"So you don't have suicidal thoughts?" he ventured.

"You're not listening to me!"

"Okay, sorry." She was right. He was listening only to parental worry. "It's funny, someone said something like that to me recently. About getting involved physically with your work."

"The woman from the grief group."

"How did you know?"

"Because I listen. She's the only one you've talked about."

"Besides your mother."

Dana looked unimpressed, and returned to Iris Chang. She told him about the web sites devoted to her, the ones trying to finger the Japanese secret services, the others that called for a boycott of Toyota products, still others that set out the secret emotional profile of Ms. Chang and blamed uncaring readers who soaked themselves in the delights of the *Rape* and its pornography of violence without understanding that Iris was drawing an excruciating self-portrait using Japanese atrocity. Her subject destroyed her. She chose it for that purpose. After her death, after the tragedy, her mother chimed in with a book that said absolutely nothing new according to Dana, who considered it a blasphemy motivated solely by profit—the Iris Chang romance was an industry as well.

Nasty stuff, but Phil was relieved to hear every word. None of this had anything to do with his daughter's projected suicide, and neither did it support his second worry. He had thought of the work she had done on the famine, and worried that Dana was fastening onto a paranoid scenario inspired by Chang, with Russian spies and their plutonium-tipped umbrellas stalking her because of the damage she had done their side with her chronicles. Even if the Ukrainian famine was established historical fact, even if dozens of books had been written about it that could be consulted in thousands of libraries, even if the studies went beyond the limits of ethnic lobbying.

He was living in his child's past, like most parents. She had gone beyond the famine. Maybe she had forgotten all about it and was absorbed by something more essential: the dangers of writing history. She was ahead of him once again. He had never considered that something bad might happen to him because of his work. When he investigated the changing nature of the rape camps of Bosnia, how they existed then disappeared, then returned to exist again, some women's groups accused him of condoning mass rape. It did not matter to them that he was investigating how a modern propaganda campaign was waged. Women denounced him on web sites he had never visited until his editor made him, but they did not call for his assassination. His editor Susan, more sensitive to those things because it was her job to be, advised him to write a short explanatory note that would run with the usual letters to the magazine to calm things down. He did what he was told, and soon another controversy supplanted his. The days of incendiary journalism were in the past.

Phil turned and put his hand on the doorknob. He was exhausted.

"Thanks for telling me about this. It's amazing the kind of stuff you know how to find."

She smiled, relieved. Her father was finally heading for the door.

"It's my job," she told him.

"You know, I read the book about Nanking."

"*The Rape of Nanking*," she corrected him.

"Yes. Of course. It's a shame she won't write another."

Phil stepped into the hallway. Poor Iris Chang, his daughter's new traumatic attachment. The attachments flew out in every direction. He badly needed a break, but there was nowhere to go.

That's when he remembered Anne Sheridan. Why hadn't he thought of her before?

Phil Brenner considered a session with Dr. Sheridan as a luxury cruise for the soul. Seeing the grief counsellor was an act of self-study, and that was the greatest work a man can do. When he walked through the door and heard the faint white noise of the dehumidifier in her basement office, it was like lapsing back into the featherbed of a childhood he had never had. Someone wanted him to feel better, someone was concerned, even if it was for a fifty-minute hour and in exchange for a substantial payment, though not a financial hardship thanks to Amy's insurance. To study the self, to be attentive to it—that was the greatest luxury imaginable. Where else were people free to linger over themselves? In many places in this world, a person with a troubled mind was pelted with stones. But in this gentle society, a man's self-study was covered by his wife's insurance. Not an infinity of visits, but sufficient to maintain his relation with Dr. Sheridan, and infrequent enough so he could go on thinking he was not really her patient.

"It has been some time," she told him as he sat down in front of her.

"Since before your party. Everyone was supposed to leave for the summer. Yet here we are, in the season of fullness."

She smiled at his lyricism as he adjusted the pillows on the chair. It was a wooden armchair softened by cushions, and it made the patient sit straight. Slouching would push the pillows onto the floor, at his feet.

"Later, I wondered about the wisdom of having that reception. Well, no harm done as far as I can tell."

It was the first time she had expressed a doubt, or let on that she might have reflected about something she'd done.

"It was a good idea. Some of us got to know each other a little better."

"Such as you and Lynne Wolfe."

"Yes."

"I hope there was no undue intimacy."

"We went out afterward for a drink at a bar in a strip mall. The Doll's House it's called, believe it or not. I don't recommend it."

"I realize intimacy occurs all the time during the process of coming to terms with loss. That's inevitable. But when potential partners can abstain, I counsel them to do so. Intimacy in a bed of loss rarely provides a positive outcome."

"We haven't been together outside of the Doll's House."

That was a lie. There was the parking lot. And his car, separated by the gearshift lever. He could live with that lie.

"A bed of loss," he repeated her words. "I suppose that's what the marriage bed has become."

"You can't expect the libido not to be tarnished by loss. Eroded. And women feel these things more strongly."

Phil leaned forward. "Are you telling me my wife is more affected by our daughter's difficulties than I am?"

"She is a woman. And so is your daughter, or will be, some day."

Despite her defence, Anne Sheridan backed off. He saw it in her manner. She straightened her back, and the effect was to pull away an inch or two from him. He had made his point. But what was hers?

"My daughter keeps changing targets. That makes her a moving target herself. First it was the Ukrainian famine. Then it was Japanese comic books. Now she's into a woman historian who killed herself, or was murdered, depending on the theory."

"Surely there is something that binds these things together."

"Anime and the Ukrainian famine. I'm afraid I haven't been able to piece them together. Not yet."

"You are spending a lot of time following her and her path. You should not forget your sense of loss, which is why you came here."

"Yes. Thanks for the reminder. But there's this terrible temptation that keeps bringing me back to my daughter. I know

I'm here for me. But I can't stay on me. I can't separate myself from her."

"Resist the temptation to play at being your daughter's therapist," she advised. "If your daughter had wanted a therapist, she would have chosen that route. As I, for one, think she should have. But you know that."

"She's involved in self-therapy. That's how she thinks of it. The women in my house aren't much for outside help. They're self-medicators."

"That's their decision. You have chosen for yourself. And by the way, self-harm and self-medicating exist, but not self-therapy."

He tried to turn away from Dana a moment, an almost impossible task. The slump, he told himself. Talk about the slump. That's about you, and about loss. Loss of ambition and energy and libido in the widest sense. But don't bother with the dream about the mummies. She doesn't like dreams, they're wrapped in wisps of Freud.

"There's a word that keeps coming back to me. Slump. As in, *I'm in a slump*. The word comes from sports."

"I didn't know that. Though I know the word, of course."

"The thing about a slump," he pursued, "is that you want to break out of it. You have to. There are any number of paths. I suppose some of them are counter-productive."

"And what have you hit on so far?"

"Work." Phil smiled guiltily. It sounded like such a male solution. "As you know, I'm casting around for a new piece, without much success. But I can't help feel that if things changed with my daughter, they would for me too."

"The solution will come from outside? From your child?"

"Yes, I know how that sounds," he admitted.

"As bad as seeking escape through ill-advised intimacy."

He raised a finger in the air. "'If you feel bad, don't do something that will make you feel worse.' Would I feel worse if I engaged in ill-advised intimacy?"

"Not to mention how your partner would feel."

They sat in silence a moment. Phil listened to the machines of Dr. Sheridan's house, the air conditioning upstairs, the dehumidifier down. He felt like a spy, or worse, a journalist, here under false pretenses, an imposture patient. He was supposed to think of himself. Instead, he thought of his daughter. His dilemma was entwined with hers, and he could not separate them.

What had happened to that sense of luxury he felt as he came up the concrete walk to her office?

He looked at Anne Sheridan. She was scribbling down notes. A judgmental therapist, which kept him at some remove from her. Perhaps that was her strategy. And a wise thing, even.

"I'm sorry." He still wanted her to like him. He still wanted to be part of the circle of favourite patients despite her hostility to his gender. "There's the speaking cure, but it looks like I'm doing the silent cure. How long have I been sitting here?"

"Who's counting? As long as you're present. As long as you're doing the work."

"At the house I interact so intensely with my daughter that sometimes I feel there's no loss at all. If I accompany her, step by step, I won't lose her."

"That is a screen activity. Many men do it."

Phil got to his feet. Can a person just walk out on his therapist? Does he not require permission, a written release to send him into the world where the solution might be?

He turned toward the door. She let him go without a

word. I am cancelling my subscription, he resolved. This is independence.

Phil Brenner envied his wife's relationship with books. Like everyone in his position, he read non-fiction for research. But he could not equal the way she gave herself to a book. She could reread one immediately after finishing it, and each time it was new to her, she found hidden aspects that emerged after the second or third reading, and revisited the characters with pleasure. Uncharitably, sometimes Phil wondered if she had really paid attention to it the first time or whether, as she did with Netflix, she was using the author to carry her into the sleep she so deeply prized.

He was jealous of the authors she slept with. He did not feel the same way about Netflix. She took her books into her bed. Netflix remained inside a box, on a screen. This evening, when she reached the end of a chapter in her book about a woman whose life was transformed by her discovery of the beauty of birds, she turned to look in his direction. He was sitting stiffly, propped up by pillows, bookless. He did not like to read in bed.

"I'm in a slump," he said.

He wanted to hear the word out loud to see how it would sound. *Slump* had begun gathering magical powers. It was becoming an independent living thing, a bad sign.

"What woman wants to hear that? Are you saying I'm not attractive?"

"That's never been a problem."

She stopped paying attention a long time ago when he told her she was beautiful, desirable, all the things men should say. Maybe she never believed him, even at the beginning. Maybe no one could believe those extravagant words at this point in life. He wasn't sure anymore. Since the scene in the parking lot, he was revising their shared past.

"I had a funny memory the other day. Actually, it was the evening I didn't have the fight with the guy in the teardown house. I remembered how when I was a teenager, I used to have these giant depressions. They came in the fall. Every fall. I don't know if it was really depression. We didn't use the word the way we do now, for everything and anything. I would get enormously frustrated. I couldn't stand myself anymore. I'd have to do something violent to break out of it."

"Violent?" Amy was briefly engaged.

"I'd go animal for a few seconds. That was the expression back then. *Go animal.* Not long, but long enough. That gave me a reputation. It turned out to be useful. I wonder where all that went."

"It could have been a teenage state. The teenage brain is a different story. Don't we know it?"

"I had a sharper, louder, more dramatic self. I've lost it."

"Not entirely," his wife told him, "by the looks of things."

"I wonder if it would even be useful these days."

His wife looked doubtful. What was truly useful now, her look said, was maintaining the routine. The routine allowed work to be done, but these days Phil's work was looking for work, and it was the toughest job out there.

"I heard a new word the other day," he told his wife, in the face of her silence. "Victimology. There was a professor on a talk show on the radio and that was his field. He taught in the department of victimology at some university. Can you believe that?"

Amy was unimpressed. Those were just words. Words came and went like teenage dance crazes. There was the mashed potato and then there was the frug and no one danced those dances anymore. No one knew how to do the watusi either. She had probably danced it and forgotten the steps. *Victimology* would meet the same fate. When it did, it wouldn't matter to her.

"It's true. You need a new project. Take your advice and find one. Or have an affair. That would be the typical thing to do. Just don't tell me about it."

"That sounds like a bad French film. This isn't France. In our world, affairs are tragic, not comic. Is that what you're doing?"

"With this body?"

"You're protesting too much. Some man will come along and make you love it again."

"I don't listen to men anymore. And I never loved my body in the first place, even when I should have."

There was a time when he treasured Amy for the way she said things like that. The old joke held its truth: a person becomes more and more herself as she gets older. He once prized her hard-headed, no-nonsense side, the way she didn't let emotions consume her, the way she stuck with one resolve. She was a communications officer at a hospital who could face down the media when there was an outbreak of *C. difficile* or a case of doctor malfeasance. With time, that side of her turned into something else. Indifference toward him, detachment when the need to please finally falls away. Was that liberation, or the antechamber of death? She could let go—had let go. Let go of him. He could not—he could not let go of anything.

Amy switched off her reading lamp and left her bird book open on the bedspread, pages thrown open, bookmark lost among the rumpled sheets. He liked birds as much as the next guy. He gathered up the book. Okay, he addressed it, change my life. Overthrow it and replace it with something better. That was a lot to ask from a bunch of birds.

Lynne called her condo *my unit* or, alternatively and more impersonally, *the unit*, which should have given Phil a hint of what he would find when he finally entered her private space. The décor of her place was a work of genius. It looked as though no one lived there, and that he was entering a model suite advertising a condo project, with Lynne playing the role of owner until the development was one hundred percent sold. Once that was done, she would move onto the next assignment, a transitory female resident for hire.

Domestic space this neutral laid a beating on Phil's stereotypes. The famous woman's touch was absent. No decorative qualities, no warm, homey nooks, no touch at all. A sadness came over Phil, sadness for her, and then for himself, for absent pleasures. *No wanting*, the neutrality said.

Lynne watched him. "You don't care for the décor," she deduced. "Not surprising."

He shrugged. "Am I so transparent?"

"Let's just say I've seen that look before. Once a man I invited over told me we should meet in a rented room, even if it cost more, because at least in a hotel the atmosphere would be warmer than here, with a restful sunset scene on the wall."

"I assume the evening didn't end happily."

Lynne said nothing, and he reconsidered the room. Its style could have belonged to some savage alternative aesthetic, or be a neo-Buddhist commentary on the vanity of accumulating things. Or maybe Lynne just didn't care about her surroundings. The result was no sense of inside.

"I'm not going to suggest we go somewhere else. Especially not the Doll's House. No, it's therapeutic here. I mean, it's like a therapist's office. Except Dr. Sheridan's has more knickknacks. Not to mention the box of Kleenex."

"Are you going to cry?

"Maybe. But not right away."

He sat on the cream-coloured sofa that would have shown the stains, had there been any. He looked into her face and understood. She let him come here so he could see her interior. It was proof that she was beyond all conventions between men and women.

But not entirely, he noted. She took out two bottles of wine, a white and a red, the same brand they drank at the Doll's House.

"I forgot who drinks what and when, so I got both."

She filled their glasses.

"I'm happy to be here."

"But we'll skip the Anne Sheridan mantras, okay?"

"Yes, please. It makes me feel like a cliché. Besides, she and I had a falling-out."

"But you were so devoted... What happened—if I may ask."

"She made sexist comments that denigrate men."

"Oh, my! How insensitive! But I'm not surprised. She's a woman, after all. She has her loyalties. And a lot of women who come to see her are there because of men."

"Agreed. But not because of me."

"Then you must be that rarest of things: a good man."

That was not a claim he was willing to make. He felt the first glass of wine slipping the weight from his shoulders, and loosening that thing that people called a *filter*, and that apparently everyone needed. If you had no filter, you were both daring and a menace.

"You spied on my husband, but then you didn't do anything. Wasn't the intelligence you gathered conclusive?"

"Your husband? You're still married?"

He would not have been surprised.

"Okay, my ex-husband. My ex. Officially ex. Happy now? But it's like the president or some other top office: it's for life. Once the husband, always the husband. A stack of divorces one on top of the other won't change that. I'll always be bound to him."

"As your daughter's father, yes, I suppose."

"As her abuser. It's a life sentence. Well, I made a choice back then. My fault. But I think they should let you go back to when you were just a girl so you can remake a few decisions."

"Isn't that what you're trying to do with Anne Sheridan?"

Lynne laughed unhappily. She shook her head. "It's all after the fact. Bolting the door, and all that."

"I thought of the sister again," Phil said. "The one he abused. Would she go public and back you up?"

Lynne laughed again, a harsh, mocking bark of a laugh. "Right. Didn't we lay that one to rest? You're so stuck in the seventies with your sisterhood."

"Okay, you win. Girls are meaner than boys. We're sentimental amateurs compared to you."

"And it gets better. The sister gave her diary to her best friend, and in it was the whole chronicle of the abuse. Blow by blow—and I mean it. And what did the best friend do? She buried the diary at the back of her underwear drawer. And why did she do that? Because the sister spurned her advances. That was her punishment for turning her down."

"The sister gave her the diary so she would divulge…"

"That's what you would normally think. But it didn't work. I guess that goes to show you. If you want a job done, you have to do it yourself."

Phil had no answer. His quest for justice was cut off at every angle. He got up from his spot on the couch and paced. That was the only positive action he could think of.

"That's rotten," he told her as if she needed telling. "It's a whole system, a family compact. It's…"

"It's the very nature of the family."

"It's a contract. And you know what? I found the contract. I found it and read it. I wanted to tell you."

Lynne was wary, but curious. She didn't ask him what the hell he was talking about. She was unsurprised by his talk of contract. She lived with irrationality every day.

"A contract for his new family, or for me?"

"Both."

"Was it written down?"

"Of course not."

"Am I guilty?" she asked.

"Absolutely not. Now I know that."

He went to her side. He took her hand and she rose to meet him so he could hold her. He thought of Bruno's mockery. *You consoled her.* There is nothing wrong with that, he told him. He put his arms around her neck and pressed his face into her hair, then against the back of her. It was like the time in the parking lot. She did not lift her arms from her sides, though he felt her become a little more holdable than that first time. What must that feel like for a woman, to be holdable? He could have asked himself the same question. Once, it was heaven. Now, he was not so sure.

She slipped out of his embrace. It did not take much effort.

"You don't have to do this, Phil. I'm not begging for a pity-fuck. And I'm not all alone."

"I'm doing it for myself."

"That's not what it feels like to me."

He was a lucky guy. He had two women in his life who were given to extreme honesty to the point of non sequitur.

117

"Dr. Sheridan called this ill-advised intimacy. Another one of her mantras."

"But it's not a new one," Lynne told him. "It's just another version of not doing something that will make you feel worse."

"You're right. But if I'm in a slump, and I want to escape it more than anything else, I might lose my sense of decorum."

"Which is just a veneer, as we all know. But please don't do it here."

Later, when the door closed behind him after the goodbye kiss, he thought of the insult to both of them: *pity-fuck*. That was the point. The starkness of the situation. You cannot go to bed with a woman after she's said *pity-fuck* to you.

As he drove home he thought of a word he half-understood, *avatar*. It was the name of a science-fiction film, but before that it meant the incarnation of a Hindu god, and then, more recently, thanks to the things computers had been made to do, it came to mean a person or thing that stands in the place of someone else. It was not a new concept. When he played Monopoly as a kid there were pieces that stood for you on the board, a car or a shoe or a top hat. You were that shoe, but of course everyone knew you weren't really a small piece of metal bent into the shape of a shoe that was keeping your spot on the board, translating your good or bad luck with the dice.

He thought of the way Lynne acted in his embrace. Maybe the nameless daughter did not exist. Her not having a name helped her not exist. She was an avatar who stood for Lynne. She *was* Lynne. What could be more normal? Something unspeakable happens to you and you shrug it off onto someone else, or shrug yourself off so the person it happened to is remarkably distant. It was probably a useful strategy until you ended up hopelessly dissociated.

TWO

A FEW DAYS LATER, the telephone rang in Phil Brenner's house. It was an untoward and welcome sound. As he reached for the phone, one of the few landlines left in existence, he briefly emerged from his exhausting hyper-vigilance over Dana, Lynne, Lynne's unnamed daughter, Megan, Amy, and everything else the world had to offer. It was his long-lost editor Susan, the one who had commissioned his Balkan pieces that aroused part of the women's movement against him. He figured she had struck him off her list because of the controversy, even if controversy is said to sell papers. Though some kinds apparently do not.

But now here he was, having a restaurant lunch with Susan, and trying to take the shallowest possible sips of wine. It was a lost cause. Magnanimous, she ordered a second glass for him. He was freelance and she was not, which meant she had an expense account, and after this lunch she had her responsibilities back at the office, and besides, if he was going back to the Balkans, he'd better bump up his drinking skills to a higher level, or the locals would massacre him.

Susan was actually going to give him work. The subject was refugees.

A number of countries in central Europe had sealed their borders to keep the exodus of displaced people off their land, which created a second crisis on top of the first. This was a violation of European Union rules about the free flow of populations, and a sign that Europe was badly fraying at the edges. The borders were strung with coils of razor wire, a reminder of the last century's grim times in the region. The closed borders set off a human backlog in the countries not trying to keep people out, either because they did not have the know-how, or they were not naturally hostile to refugees. Serbia was one of those countries. Refugees were allowed to enter the country freely from the south, and they were expected to head north into Europe. The blocked borders changed all that.

"I figure you're the right one to look into the situation. Have you kept in touch with people there?" Susan asked.

"I still have my contacts. They don't go away. People are very faithful in that place. That's one of the reasons I love it."

And to prove his continuing relation with the country, he launched into an anecdote. There was a broad, spacious park in downtown Belgrade that had swelled with men, and a few women and children, busy washing out their socks and waiting for something to give. One day a group of ladies of the night approached them, full of solicitude and not wanting to offend, and afraid of offending because they knew nothing about the refugees' ways except that pork was out of the question. The women worked the park at night, and had done so long before the refugees arrived. They had pooled part of their earnings to buy a pair of heavy-duty bolt-cutters that they had wrapped in a burlap sack, not namby-pamby wire-cutters, but a real survival tool. They offered the cutters to a group of tense, idle men consulting their mobile phones. The women pointed north. *Hungary. Frontier. Fence. Cut.* One of them made a cutting motion with her fingers. She was the one who could speak the best English, the universal language of refugees.

"Now, that story might not be absolutely true," Phil admitted to Susan. "Though if it isn't, it should be."

She rewarded him with a thin smile. He understood his mistake, too late. It was the whores. She did not appreciate anecdotes in which women were degraded, even if they were doing something noble and generous.

He was surprised, not only that Susan was bringing him back into her fold, but that she was sending him to do a piece on refugees in the Balkans. That was an amazing turnaround. She hadn't given him work since the beginning of the century, or almost, and now she was sending him back to Serbia, where he had not been since Milošević fell. He had been in the Belgrade crowd cheering on the backhoe as it bulldozed through the front door of the Parliament. Suddenly the Serbs were not bad guys anymore. They were friends of the refugees. The bad guys, who used to be good guys, were now in the countries north and west of Serbia, a barrier between refugees and salvation in Europe.

"The locals are friendly enough to the refugees, that's what I've heard," Phil told her, as if he were in contact with the place on a daily basis, "but none of them wants to stay there. Unemployment is at twenty-five percent, if not more. The country is just a stop along the way."

Susan watched him fiddle with his empty wine glass. Two glasses were all her expense account would provide.

"Go to the refugee centres and the borders," she told him. "Find out what relations are like, especially since in Bosnia, it was hardly smooth sailing between Muslims and Serbs. And now here come all these Muslim refugees. Get the pulse of what the population is thinking. Are they attacking them, or are they love-bombing them? Your fence-cutter story with the ladies of the night is charming, but let's go beyond it."

"The Serbs see themselves as refugees. And a lot of them are, or have been. So they have empathy." Phil shook his head in wonderment. "This is a dream assignment. I appreciate it, Susan."

"I know it is, for you. I'm happy to provide the chance. Those people over there are your people."

"I don't exactly come from the Balkans."

"I know that. But immigrants, refugees—they're your thing."

"They're everybody's thing these days. Including your magazine's."

She gave him a smile fashioned for the circumstances. She did not have to win the argument by logic. She was hiring him, and that was victory enough for her.

"Just remember to come back. Your wife would kill me if I sent you on a story and you decided to go native and not return."

"I don't think she'd get that upset."

"Actually, I don't want to know about it."

Susan called for the bill as he made a show of trying to pay. Instructions would follow in an e-mail: the number of words, honorarium, travel allowance, the usual. The magazine's agency would arrange the tickets. She was already working an app on her phone to call a taxi.

In front of the restaurant, he watched her move toward the waiting car. Modest heels, pleated skirt on the short side, stockings despite the last hurrah of summer. They had slept together back when they were both just starting out.

She turned to him as he held the car door open.

"I like using you, Brenner, in spite of yourself."

Then she was gone.

He remembered one of his nights with Susan. The rendez-vous took place on a pleasure craft among a row of similar models in the harbour. He was a nervous young suitor and very eager to please, and as the evening went on without too much affect from her end, the sting of failure, which he was always quick to feel, urged him into counter-productive fretting. He ended up losing her the way he had lost other women, with a smothering overabundance of attention. He suspected her of setting up the date on a friend's boat essentially to draw a picture of herself spending a night with a man on water, him or another, it made little difference. He was part of the furniture, the set. As he wooed her prior to their descending into the cabin, he imagined her describing the scene to her girlfriends, with the intimate details excised, of course, since they might not be too glorious, and women like Susan did not admit to such things. Phil was not exactly a master of the secrets of the human heart back then, but he did sense that much. He must have turned in an average performance below decks, and she declined to repeat the exercise the next morning when they awoke in the gently rocking craft. When he urged her to give in to his attempts at tenderness, she struck back. "With you, there's always *something!*"

Those words, her exasperated tone, had stayed with him till this day. Everything else had faded but his sense of failure. I must have been a dismal lover, he concluded. But was it me, or was it her? *Both* would be the only fair assessment. Women did not do much in bed back then, at least not the ones willing to have him. They received his attentions as if they were their due, in an abstract way, outside their bodies, looking on from above, or slightly to one side. Their way of being unnerved him. His reaction was to do too much.

Dismal was the verdict he pronounced on himself.

After she left, he stood on the sidewalk in front of the restaurant. That she was willing to hire him again was a tribute to how little that night mattered to her, then and now. The whole time, she had probably been taking notes on the nautical decor.

He walked toward his car a couple blocks away, on a street where the parking was free.

Phil had not entered Dana's sanctuary for a number of days, not since the Iris Chang episode. He had read *The Rape of Nanking* once, and since he did not reread books, he thought it was solidly in the past. That turned out not to be true. It continued to pursue him. If you won't read me, I'll read you, it mocked him. But I did read you, he protested. Iris—like his daughter he was suddenly on first-name basis with a dead woman he had never met—had made a chance discovery, the journal of a German civilian who had tried to rescue people in the city, and it opened up the gates of history's horrors for her. But of course there was no such thing as chance for writers of this kind of material. They had to be in a state of readiness, receptivity, though it did not have to be conscious. They needed to be attentive to the world's atrocities, especially the ones no one knew about and that had not yet been turned into Hollywood movies. Chang's work was admirable. It was a shame there would be no more from her. If you have written a book that good and that essential, how could you put an end to yourself? But she had, and in grand symbolic style. Self-death was a mystery to him. How people contrived to leave this world and all its unpredictable chaos and beauty was one more thing Phil could not fathom. *Fathom* was the word for it. It meant journeying to a depth he fortunately could not reach.

Dana was on her bed in overalls, a T-shirt, and gym shoes. He did not get the bit with the shoes. Was she about to go jogging? A flock of three-by-five cards was scattered across the bedspread. He picked one up. The famine was back. It had pushed Iris Chang off the page.

"Where do you find those cards? I haven't seen them since the last century. They used to rule the world, but computers eliminated them."

"I get them at the vintage shop. You can relive your whole misspent youth there if you have the cash. They have all kinds of stuff from your time. Even typewriters."

"I had three typewriters. An Olympia, an Olivetti, and a Brother. I think they're still in the basement somewhere. I loved each one of them. They each had a personality. Writing was physical then. It's easier to write when it's physical." He held up his hands, fingers spread. "I used to type so hard I'd get blood blisters on my fingertips."

"Vintage shop," his daughter said brightly, as if those words were a magic formula that would solve his problems with aging.

"I'll remember that. Maybe they'll even have ribbons." Dana looked at him quizzically. "Typewriter ribbons," he explained. "For typing on typewriters."

"They have everything old."

"Not old," he corrected her. "Vintage."

"No. Old. Vintage means people want to buy it. Sometimes old is just old."

"Thanks for the clarification." There was no sense arguing with a young person. "Listen, Dana, I have good news for once. I finally got a job. I mean, the kind I've been looking for. I'm going on a research trip. And you know, I had this crazy thought. You could come with me, either part of the time or all of it." He held up a card as if it were a piece of evidence, an exhibit for the one-girl jury. "You'd be closer to the zone that interests you."

"I don't have to go there. Why would I want to?"

"Don't you want to hear nightingales first-hand?"

"What nightingales? What are you talking about?"

"You don't remember?"

Phil stopped himself. He would have sworn, not too long in the past, certainly close enough for him to remember, that they had had a conversation about nightingales and hedgehogs. The hedgehogs weren't the issue, the birds were, he had praised their song and told Dana one day he would take her to hear them. It had clearly been more important to him than her.

"You should come with me," he said, pushing the night-ingale question aside. "These work trips are lonely once the rush is over. You'll make it more fun."

"Me, fun?"

"Of course you're fun! You don't see yourself like that, but you are. Look at all the stuff we talk about. I would have never heard of Iris Chang without you. Or the other things, those drawings. You make my world bigger."

"Mom might not let me go. She's jealous. It would get worse if I went, and you'd end up paying."

"How could she be jealous? We're both your parents."

His question hung in the air with all its ludicrous naïveté, like so many things he said. Amy, jealous. His wife was never jealous. There was a time when he wished she were. Then the word widened out from the simple way he and most people used it, as a feeling of sexual anxiety. It was about the claim parents could make on their children's affections.

He looked up, into Dana's face. Her lips were trembling as if she were about to speak. He waited, but nothing came.

"Your mother, jealous. I wouldn't have imagined."

"Come on, go ahead, you can figure it out."

My daughter is brilliant, he realized, once again. She knows that in this house she's the battleground, we capture and then we lose the territory that is the affection and knowledge of who she is beyond her simple place in the family. If he took a trip with her, he would be making enormous gains on the terrain of her heart and soul, he would live bravely with her disorders, far from the resources they had here.

But only if things worked out. That was not guaranteed. The trip might turn out to be intolerable for both of them. He was ready to take that chance. But Amy, left behind with their well-adjusted child who did not seem to need her parents, might not approve.

She would not approve, he understood. But how much would she oppose the trip?

"I can see the little wheels turning," Dana told him. "You're thinking about what I said."

"Yes. It completely surprised me. But it makes sense. Which is why you should make the trip. But do it for me, not to spite your mother."

"Don't make me laugh! I get it completely. You want to make Mom jealous. You're something else. You're just like any kid. I had a boyfriend once who tried to do the same thing. It didn't work."

The next day, Phil spent money he had not made yet on a plane ticket that matched the times and destinations of the one Susan's magazine provided. Amy took the news with some incredulity, but she did not try to stop his plan. A long time ago, at the beginning, they swore they would not let Dana separate them. That was one of their many impossible promises.

Phil and Dana reversed their roles on the first leg of the trip, the flight over the Atlantic to Paris. He turned to Ativan to ward off the near-claustrophobia he developed in planes. He knew the feeling well; he had been in a lot of planes. Dana took the opposite position. "The only way I can do this is if I'm clear-headed. I mean, as much as I can be." When the flight attendant presented her with a plastic goblet of wine, she took one sip, made a face and handed it over to Phil. He was happy for the additional dose.

Dana watched him empty the goblet. He saw disapproval in her eyes.

"Sorry, I suffer from travel anxiety," he told her. "The more I travel, the worse it is. You would have thought I would have gotten used to it by now. But don't worry, I always come through on the other side."

It was embarrassing to confess a weakness to his daughter, but worse, he calculated, to say nothing. The drugs were a gift from Bruno. Phil had asked as casually as he could manage, and he gave him twice what he wanted. "I never go out of the house without them," Bruno said, and dug into the pocket of his sports jacket.

Until he spoke to invite Dana on this trip, he hadn't known that was what he wanted, and he didn't consider his next move if Amy had said no. Her disapproval never coalesced into refusal. Sitting in the plane next to Dana, he was almost giddy with the newness of it, even through the veil of the hypnotic drug. It occurred to him, though it was too late, that he might have skipped the drugs and stayed up with his daughter, and been attentive and available if she needed him. But there would be time enough on the slow Balkan roads. Some of Bruno's drug supply might end up going to her if the demands of travel were too much. His daughter who never left her room—part of him still believed that, even if it was patently false. At her feet was her latest acquisition from the vintage shop, a well-worn briefcase bought during one of her forays he had thought she never engaged in. With her load of papers, she looked like a young professor off to some conference on literary theory in Paris, the city that had long been the capital of obscurantism.

He closed his eyes. A tense bon-voyage glass of wine with Amy before she drove them to the terminal, drinks at the airport bar and sour domestic wine on the plane laid on top of Bruno's gift Ativan. Through the veil of those substances that should not be combined, as everyone knew, he thought back to his two going-away conversations. Both were full of the standard regrets.

First, there was Megan. He went down the stairs to her basement hideout to announce the trip. He thanked her for the Beauchard book again, and described how he had devoured it in one long night's sitting, all three hundred pages or more, and had paid for the experience with a pitiless case of insomnia. He tried to let her know that he understood the message she was sending with the book, but he was not particularly successful. When you can't find the right words to say something, it probably means you should keep your mouth shut. It was risky, and bad parenting on top of it, to attribute intentions to your child that she might not have, or might not know she had.

After that stumbling attempt, he told her he was taking her older sister to the Balkans.

"I knew it. She's your favourite," Megan said. "Your favourite daughter."

"We don't play favorites here."

He got a smile of disbelief. "You stood in the emergency line at the passport office for her. Mom told me."

"Sometimes we have to make extra efforts for certain people." He looked around the room, the unmade bed and the little vial of perfume that must have been a gift from the phantom boyfriend. "Wouldn't you rather be you than her?"

Megan shrugged. "Sure. But she's still your favourite."

"In families, that's not always an enviable position."

"Don't worry, Dad, I know that. And you've said it too. *You brung yourself up yourself.* Your mother told you that once, when you were an adult. You seemed pretty proud, but really, you weren't happy at all."

Megan was as brilliant as Dana, both girls were brilliant in their own way, with the intelligence they had developed to live in this family that was not so bad after all, he thought, there were many worse. He was proud of them both, though more a companion to Dana. Megan was a teenager living in a basement, a typical teenage choice, perhaps, but she wasn't self-absorbed like most girls her age. She could see that the resilience her father developed from bringing himself up by himself was essential at the time, and maybe still useful as an adult, but the fruit of trauma she did not have to face.

"Have a good trip. And come back in one piece. Both of you."

He held her for a moment. Then, relieved, he moved upstairs to pack.

He adjusted his cramped body on the unforgiving synthetic fabric of the airplane seat. For a moment he wished he was flying back home, and not away, out into the unstable world. He made that wish every trip. It was simple insecurity, the famous travel anxiety that must be overcome every time, like stage fright. Next to him, Dana sat unmoving. Maybe she was meditating. He wouldn't have put it past her.

At the end of that conversation, Megan said one more thing that returned to him now. He cursed himself. He was terminally slow. Often he did not react to what people told him until hours or days later.

"You know, sometimes I tease her about being half-mental. I figure it's good for her. She'll feel, like, more part of the family. More normal. No need for kid gloves or anything."

Phil would have given anything to have that moment back. Megan, teasing her older sister about her disorders—how would she have done that? Behind it, he believed, there was love, as often there is with family teasing. Megan wanted her sister to get better. That's what *normal* meant. Normal like she was, loving life, not all the time, maybe, but at least *in* life. He couldn't remember the last time he heard Megan and Dana have a conversation. There was more going on in his house than he knew.

Then Megan astonished him further.

"Everyone thinks I'm so strong. I'm like you, bringing yourself up. Well, if I was so strong, I'd take on Dana's condition, whatever it is. I'd take it on and beat it, I'd beat the absolute shit out of it, and she'd be free, and you'd have your favourite daughter back."

It was the kind of thing someone will tell you just before goodbye.

The second conversation was with Amy. Her voice was over-poised and brittle. He heard her wanting this to be over.

"Dana is fragile. Don't do anything to aggravate her condition."

"If we only knew what her condition was. All these diagnoses, and none of them seems right to me. What classification does she really belong in—if any?"

"She has anorexic tendencies and a borderline personality.

She's obsessive. You should know that by now."

"Those are just names for things. You sound like the DSM. Diagnoses come and go, and most of the time they're misdiagnoses because they're based on fashion."

"So taking her to some place where people are more miserable than she is—that's your idea of helping?"

Phil performed a little exercise he did when he had the presence of mind to, in the midst of one of these sterile domestic exchanges that made it impossible to recognize the woman he loved. He stepped back. He dissociated, but for a good cause. He looked at his wife carefully, her hands, her hair, how her clothes spoke for the shape of her body—for the lack of shape, she would say now. He listened to her attentively. What was she saying?

You're not taking my daughter. I need her too much.

All right, he thought. That's fair.

"We'll be back before you know it," he told her. "She'll be yours again. And she'll be better than ever, I promise."

His words made her turn away and leave the room.

Hold me in your arms, he appealed to Morpheus who he hoped was sitting in a row not too far away. Deliver me. Love me a little, but not too long and not too hard. Just a time out, that's all I want. Haven't I earned it?

But Phil got his gods wrong. Morpheus is the god of dreams, and the son of Hypnos, the god of sleep. He was talking to the son when he should have been talking to the father. With the chemicals at work in his mind, there would be no dreams.

Phil Brenner awoke when the wheels hit the runway at the Roissy airport, stunned to be anywhere at all with his pasty mouth and the sense that he had lost a night out of his life. There was a reason why they told you not to mix Ativan and wine. The sky was grey as it always is in Paris, the leaden cover that keeps the cigarette smoke and diesel fumes hanging low over the rooftops of the city. Dana was sitting, still unmoving, eyes open, looking forward, just the way he had left her when the self-medicating kicked in. He felt his cowardice and the embarrassment over it. Maybe it's not such a good idea to travel with your child. You expose yourself. A man should be able to take a flight without rendering himself unconscious. In the rows he could see, half the passengers were asleep with their heads and limbs at impossible angles, unmoved by the PA system's welcome message. The use of hypnotics was widespread.

The Belgrade flight left from a terminal with a third-world feel, outside the ideal space of the Schengen Agreement, where the Balkan-bound departures were lined up, ready to jet off to the history-worn capitals of the new republics. In that part of the world, the notion of "country" was being reinvented every day. Phil and Dana held tickets on Air Serbia, an airline owned by the Arabs. Its name had been changed from Jugoslavia Air Transport, since the country had not existed for decades. But the joke lived on. The pilots were very skilled, since they had had countless hours of experience flying in the wars of the 1990s. They could handle anything, even civil aviation.

The sodden, post-medication weight on his brain had Phil dozing in the departure lounge after a second passage through security screening, a special JAT touch complete with more X-rays and a hand search of their bags without benefit of gloves, though they had not left the quarantined zone of the airport. Before they set out, he had wondered what he and Dana would talk about on this long trip. Not much, it turned out.

In the discomfort of a straight-backed chair, Phil recalled the last time he was in Paris, a few years back. He and Amy spent two weeks in "intimate" Paris, as she put it. They would visit no museums or monuments. They would explore gardens and courtyards and see the backstage of the city, while other people saw only the façade. And of course they would visit shops where fashionable and creative clothing was sold. They did not form a financial union, so when he pulled out his credit card in a dress shop, it meant something. He was ready to buy her whatever she liked, and he told her so.

He pictured a scene from that trip: Amy standing in front of a rack of clothing in a fashionable ladies' store on the rue de Turenne, the sleek salesgirl praising the outfits in English in her delightful accent, and Amy paying her no attention. His wife picked the dress he knew she would, the one he had his eye on from the start. The most expensive one, no doubt, or at least he hoped so. He wanted to spoil her. They were on a trip to Paris without the girls. This was their time.

Amy held up the dress and admired it. Then she pressed it against her body, modelling it. Her expression changed entirely. She looked crestfallen—that antiquated word came to him. As if she were proudly wearing a mantle, a crown, some queenly, womanly finery, and it had tumbled to the floor.

She replaced the dress on the rack.

"I can't wear things like that anymore."

She turned and went out the door, leaving him to apologize to the salesgirl.

He caught up to her on the sidewalk, and made the mistake of saying he would have gladly bought the dress for her, as if money were the issue. But she already had a closet full of pretty things he gave her and that she never put on.

Which made her stroll across the strip mall parking lot all the more striking.

Then Dana was shaking him awake.

"Come on, I can't believe you can sleep in a chair. They're announcing last call. You want to go on this trip with me or not?"

The Tourism Faculty used the Hotel Palace as its training ground, but it did not seem that the students had much of a future in the industry. Or that the industry had any future in Belgrade. Or maybe it was the resolutely musty atmosphere of the Palace; the fun people stayed elsewhere. Before the country of Yugoslavia split up in violent divorce, Belgrade had the reputation for throwing the best parties in Europe.

Maybe the staff was still hungover from those days. They seemed to have attended several other faculties before coming to rest in hotel management and tourism—perhaps they had flunked out of demolition school. Most of the men were of indeterminate age, somewhere between thirty-five and fifty, with their tight mouths, buzz cuts, and bullet-shaped skulls. It was hard to tell, in this place people aged differently. They were clearly unaccustomed to the company of women, and unable to grasp the relation between Dana and Phil. They assumed she was his wife, and when he introduced her as his daughter they laughed, as if sharing a locker-room joke. Maybe they suffered from relationship blindness. They seemed to have no family but each other, and no independent existence outside the hotel. They lived on the mezzanine level, in a wing of their own.

Phil had stayed at the Palace a dozen years ago or more, in more troubled times than these, and the staff remembered him. There was not a lot of job mobility in the city. Those were the days when he was the only Westerner in Belgrade. Back then the men would do anything for him, and it was a struggle to get the bartender to take his money at the end of the evening.

Here, the laws of hospitality outweighed those of capital. Then again, profit was not a motive at the Palace. Since it was a university faculty, the hotel and everything inside it belonged to the government, and that included the staff.

Walking into the lobby with Dana after the taxi ride snapped Phil out of his lethargy. He loved the oddities of the Palace, and he pointed them out to Dana, who was less appreciative. The money-changing robot in the lobby that looked like a vending machine, and gave the best rates in town, even better than the Piranha currency exchange around the corner. The Aperitiv Bar in the lobby with its dusty, homemade bottles of fruit brandy that simultaneously triggered and cured hangovers. Phil's greatest affection was for the Bakelite telephones. In the room, after checking in and promising the staff to come down for a drink as soon as possible, he held the handset to his nose. The apparatus gave off a slightly fishy odour.

He demonstrated the phenomenon for Dana.

"I don't have to smell it. I believe you." She looked at the narrow bed with its worn coverlet. "Though it's vintage for sure."

She took out her phone and photographed the room from a variety of angles. Then she took a picture of the view out the window, a forest of antennae and chimneys over red tile roofs. Is this going to end up in her stories, Phil wondered, but that would have been the absolute worst question to ask. A story was something made up, invented, something fake, and that was the traditional charge against people with disorders: they were making them up to attract attention, or because they were slackers.

Dana went and sat on the bed with her chin in her palms. He felt jetlag descending on her. That was the advantage of the drug once the body expelled it on this side of the Atlantic. A person could launch into work immediately. Phil left his daughter to nap, and went to his room to get on the phone. Quickly, he was back in his element: the search, the chase, giving to get, being professionally empathetic. This part of the world, inexplicably, had always been good to him, even as it seemed to curse the actual inhabitants.

That evening he took Dana to Vuk, an outdoor restaurant close to the Palace, in the pedestrian zone, the closest thing to European elegance Belgrade could offer. It stood facing a slot club—a mini-casino. "Vuk," Phil said, meant "wolf," and it was also the first name of the historian of the Serbian language, Vuk Karadžić. There was the bad Karadžić, the one who ended up at the International Penal Tribunal in The Hague, and there was the good one, Vuk, who studied and systemized his unruly native tongue.

Dana looked around the sidewalk café and at the indolently strolling citizens passing by, many of whom, Phil knew, were carrying automatic pistols.

"It's just like Paris," she said, "not that I've ever been there. But I'm still dead tired. How do you do this—all this travelling?"

"Adrenaline. And experience."

"Now I get the business with the pills. I see I'm not the only user in the family."

"You can add your mother to the list too."

"I texted her so she won't die of jealousy."

"What did you say to soothe her?"

"I told her I was in a ghetto room with a crummy view and a bed with itchy sheets and a telephone that smells like fish."

Phil laughed. "That might not work. You make it sound exotic."

The waiter brought the mixed grill. If Dana decided to be a vegetarian tonight, she could eat the salad around it. And

139

if she decided to eat nothing, he'd eat for two. Tonight he was on vacation from vigilance, it was time out, he would live for himself. That was the first glass of Macedonian merlot talking, urging disinhibition, joining hands with every glass of wine he had taken in his life. Sometimes he saw it that way: a long chain of glasses hand in hand, even if glasses have no hands, stretching through outer space, all the way to the moon or further if necessary, a link to distant galaxies.

He set a matching pair of cutlets on her plate.

"When I was here years ago, there was a show at the modern art museum. I was covering it because one of our artists was invited, a high-concept guy with a shaved head named Fahrat. We were in a fancy restaurant way swankier than here with bodyguards smoking outside, the embassy was paying for it. The waiter came to take the order and the artist told him, 'I'm a vegetarian.' 'I am sorry to hear that,' the waiter said very mournfully. 'So, you will have the mixed grill?'"

"The refusal to eat meat is an indicator of sexual anxiety," Dana declared.

"Really? Why would that be?"

"You know. Meat. Taking flesh in your mouth."

Phil laughed before he could stop himself. Dana was a brilliant girl, but what she knew about the world of sex came from web sites. She gave him a withering teenage look.

"Mom told me she was having an affair."

The merlot upswing and the warm early autumn air fell away. He turned cold, which happened to him when grand emotion was called for. He felt the familiar alliance, just as unpleasant this second time: the blending of his wife and his daughter, a joining of their bodies.

"Now why would she tell you that?"

And why are you repeating it? he thought. Did you freely agree to participate in this proxy war?

Dana shrugged. "I don't know. I don't even know if it's true. Maybe I was supposed to think she was glamorous, and get interested in how exciting being a woman is. She freaked out when I said I wasn't menstruating."

"I can understand."

"I know all about what an affair is, but only from the movies. It's supposed to be dashing and dangerous. You can get your rabbit cooked."

"And worse," Phil assured her.

Dana looked up at him. "I said the wrong thing."

"There's no right or wrong thing," he answered carefully. "When someone says something to us, especially if it's a major revelation that we haven't asked for, we never know if they're telling the truth, not at first. All we can hope to understand is why they're telling us."

He turned his attention to the grilled meat. Dana was a brilliant girl, so why would she let herself be used in such a transparent way—unless, in her immaturity, she had no real sense of what an affair meant to a marriage. That's what he wanted to know: whether Amy had made Dana her messenger, accidentally or otherwise. He couldn't ask. And he never would. He would do what his wife had not done, though they had agreed to it many times, and that was to keep Dana and Megan out of their private life. Of course there was no such thing as private life when you lived under the same roof. But there was minding your own business in a judicious fashion, and not ruining your children's existence by leaving the bedroom door open.

Amy is jealous of this trip. Dana said it first. Amy is trying to make me jealous in turn. And succeeding, he admitted as he chewed his food. It was a crude strategy, something out of high school, but judging how tasteless the food suddenly felt on his tongue, it had done its job. These old tricks always worked. A shame, because the meat was always good in the Balkans, the animals free to roam and graze, they weren't stamped out in the mechanized production that delivered portion-controlled servings onto the plates in his country. The meat was delicious, though always overcooked. Balkan people had a fear of blood in their food. But right now the pleasure was gone.

He signalled the waiter for another half-litre of merlot. He felt bad, and was about to do something that might make him feel worse. Anne Sheridan sat on his shoulder, her feminist, *tsk-tsk* finger moving back and forth like a solar-powered hula girl on the dashboard of a car. Screw off, he told her, you don't know anything about men's emotions. You don't even believe they have any.

The waiter served Dana first with careful attention and a showy twist of the carafe. *Così fan tutte*, Phil thought, the school for lovers. Thus do they all. Amy told him to have an affair, at least he thought she had, though the merlot rendered that memory iffy. Everything was making perfect sense now, always a dangerous sign. A man would come along and teach her to love her body again. Her body an old garment, she claimed, as forlorn as the tattered coat in the song. When it came to him, yes.

He looked up at Dana. She was chewing her meat slowly, assimilating it fibre by fibre.

"Tomorrow a friend is taking me to a shelter for immigrants. You'll come with."

"What will I do?"

"Talk to them. Take notes. What you always do. What I'll be doing. It's better if there are two sets of ears. We can compare afterwards."

"I don't know their language."

"There's always someone who speaks some English."

"I don't know. I'm afraid."

Phil reached out and took Dana's hand. He was back on familiar ground. It felt good. He was her father, he was comforting her, urging her along, he was a little solicitous but that was one of his chronic faults that apparently she accepted, it didn't matter if Amy had had an affair or not, or was still having one at this very moment, with the time difference it would have been afternoon delight. The surprise of hearing the word *affair* in his daughter's mouth had thrown him. What was it doing there, so incongruous, who had put it there? What did having an affair mean to Dana? *You can get your rabbit cooked.*

This trip was opening his eyes, and it was barely Day One.

Once they left Vuk, not overly late because this was Belgrade, not Paris, they still had to wait some minutes at the locked front door of the Palace. In the end, an employee lurched into view, conjuring up the Addams Family. It was the same employee who took Dana for his wife.

"*Dobro noc*," Phil attempted.

"Pretty good for a foreigner," the employee complimented him. "What else can you say?"

"*Jasam stari pisac.*"

The man frowned. "Be careful with that last word. You almost said 'pussy.'"

Dana laughed loudly. She was still laughing as they climbed the stairs with its worn carpet. Puffs of dust rose with every step.

"I loved the way he said 'pussy.' If a guy said it to me with that accent, I'd give him mine."

"This certainly is the evening of frank talk."

143

They stood in front of the door to her room.

"Are you going to call up Mom and yell at her?"

"Yelling at people usually doesn't work."

"What does work? I'd like to know."

Phil breathed out, exhausted. *Nothing*, he felt like saying. But that wasn't an answer a father gives his daughter.

"Patience," he told her.

Dana looked disappointed. She was too young for patience. She turned the heavy antique key and went into her vintage room where her night's labour awaited her.

In his room, Phil sat down at what passed for a desk at the Palace, a shelf that jutted out of the wall. He roused his computer. The Palace's WIFI network was waiting for him. He thought of Lukács's Marxist bon mot describing the Frankfurt School of leftist philosophers: the Grand Hotel Abyss, where nothing works but the plumbing. In this case it was the WIFI. He used it to send Amy a bread-and-butter message: *Arrived, all well except for jetlag, though it did not keep D. and I from having a good talk.*

His wife's answer to his message came as he was pouring the last unnecessary helping of duty-free Calvados from the Paris airport into a plastic cup. She assumed Dana had carried the mail, the *good talk* they had had, because there was no message at all, no explanation because none was necessary, just four scans painfully slow to download on the hotel network. When they finally opened, he recognized the watermarked paper that served as the background. On her last birthday, at a loss for gift ideas now that clothes and perfume and every other feminine vanity were out of the question, he gave Amy an elegant leather-bound blank book. A diary, a space where she could note down her thoughts away from the pragmatism of her job. Here was his birthday gift, returned to sender. If you give your wife a blank book, you are inviting her to fill it. You can't expect to like what you will receive in return. The pages had been waiting for this moment, like the obituary of a famous person whose death has long been imminent.

I did not expect Dana to talk. She is so terribly prudish. I am amazed she did. Unless you coaxed it out of her. You are always trying to get inside her head.

I wouldn't have told you. When I was young, I learned how to lie. It is a useful skill that soon turns into a habit. Anyway, I didn't need to lie, you never asked.

I know you'll want details. How long has it been going on? That's the first question husbands ask. They want to know how long their wives have been able to accomplish the feat of keeping them from knowing. A while. A good while, actually. Long enough to make me wonder where it is going, and how long we can sustain it, and what the real point of it is. He is married too. I assume he is still making love to his wife, though he says he isn't. Those calculations were important to me at the beginning. Then I stopped thinking about it. He doesn't ask me, though I know he is jealous. Don't placate him, he once said to me about you. After a while he stopped quizzing me. The subject is not very glorious, and you never really get the truth.

I figured it would go on for a while, then collapse under its own weight, the bother and effort of it, the repetition.

But it didn't. So that makes it not an affair anymore. It is something else. It is a relationship, perhaps my primary one.

He hasn't made me love my body, the way you said some man would. I smiled to myself when you said that. He loves my body, or at least he says he does, so I don't have to. That's what matters. He has freed me from that pre-occupation.

Maybe it's better that you're far away, and absorbed in something new. You are busy, and in any case we are not going to have a trans-Atlantic argument over this issue. Don't do anything foolish. Don't take risks. Our daughters still need their father. You will come back, and we will see.

That was Amy through and through. An innovator when it came to the art of confession. She knew how the Internet worked in these countries. How her message would open slowly on the screen, line by painful line, like a striptease, allowing him slow and gradual access to a truth he would have guessed after the first line on any high-speed system. He thought of her rejection line about wanting to be reassured without having to do anything. She was a genius. He was surrounded by genius women.

Amy was right. The question of *when* was a real one. It concerned vanity, which always arises in cases like this. How long had he been living with a stranger? Forever?

Stranger? Some part of him had been waiting for this. Some part of him had been aware since the day in the parking lot. But there is knowing, and then there is knowing that you know, and they are far from being the same thing. A shock is necessary to bring the two together.

Phil was working on his whole grilled red pepper, a Balkan breakfast staple in early autumn, when Dana came in. The hotel had felt deserted the previous evening, but it turned out not to be. A good number of tables were filled with guests, locals who did not bother removing the seeds from their peppers the way he did. Dana slid onto the chair next to him and looked at his plate.

"Vegetables for breakfast. Sounds healthy."

"The buffet has everything. Stock up, we don't know where our next meal is coming from."

Dana didn't mention what she had let slip the evening before, if indeed it was an accident. Phil did not expect her to return to the subject. It was his to dwell on, not hers. Parents' emotions are rarely real for their children. That is as it should be. She came back from the buffet with her plate and he watched her eat. As she pushed her food around with her fork, trying to figure out what it was, wondering why she was eating raw garlic and clotted cream for breakfast, she looked like a perfectly normal teenage girl faced with the unfamiliar. That was part of his plan, along with hoping to ward off his own loneliness. He wanted to take her out of her room and her house where she was the star of her disorder, and cast her into the wonderful harsh vastness of the shared world. And Amy had used his plan to deliver her opaque message.

No, not opaque. It was so coolly reasonable it could have been written by a psychopath. There was not an emotion anywhere in it. How could someone with no emotions have an affair? But emotion was there somewhere behind her words, and she owed him nothing. He looked across the table at Dana. This trip would bring communion, if it didn't bring disaster. It was the kind of ill-advised, high-risk strategy Dr. Sheridan would have steered him away from. But something had happened to the grief counsellor. She was no longer there, perched on his shoulder.

Dana breathed out a cloud of fresh garlic and looked at her fork. "Pretty strong stuff for breakfast."

"It'll stay with you till the next dose. It's elemental."

"Meaning what?"

"Crude but necessary. The basic building blocks of life."

Dana smiled.

The Pančevo refugee camp was northeast of the city, in a grade school that had fallen on hard times and been largely abandoned. The zone had been bombed in the dying days of the twentieth century because a fertilizer plant was located there, and fertilizer contains nitrogen that can be used in bomb-making, or so ran NATO logic at the time. Once the factory was put out of commission, and the area hopelessly contaminated, the workers left the district, taking their children with them. There were only a few left, the offspring of families who did not have the mobility or strength to move somewhere else or who, incredibly, had not heard the news.

Phil and Dana were standing in front of the heavy wooden doors of the Palace when a copper-coloured PT Cruiser pulled up. It was the only one of its kind in town. The driver jumped out. It was amazing how a man that large could fit into that cartoon car with its retro lines. It was Dragan, one of Phil's first contacts in the country who had become a friend in the meantime through various shared ordeals. Dragan had gone from being a useful local, a fixer tinged with madness but generally trustworthy, into a moral touchstone, someone he returned to often in his thoughts, a man who accompanied him from afar through the decisions of his life. A Balkan version of Bruno, but with greater energy, whose cynicism was more tender, more creative. He spotted Phil by the hotel doors and pointed showily at his watch.

"Analytical hours!" he shouted proudly.

That was the expression he adopted to point to his ability to arrive exactly on time, a rare performance in the Balkans. He must have been in some therapeutic relationship at one point, or knew someone who was, since he understood that being late, even by a minute, would be subject to savage interpretation. Dragan's English was a tasty stew of formality from book learn-ing and humour born of non sequitur, punctuated by expressions like *grand* and *swell* learned from old American films.

"You are a true psychiatrist, not a second late," Phil compli-mented him, and they embraced. "Either that, or a patient."

"No, not a patient. I am your psychiatrist! That means you are in trouble of a profound nature!"

He got around to noticing Dana. In this part of the world, friendship between men was primal, and the rest more or less frills.

"So you have gotten married again. Congratulations are in order!"

"This is my daughter Dana," Phil said.

"I should be embarrassed, maybe, but I am not."

Dana shook his hand. "You're the second person who said I'm my father's wife. Is there something I don't know?"

"Ah, us men here, we suffer from age blindness. We should get better glasses. More age-appropriate ones. Now, let's make tracks."

149

He opened the doors of the Cruiser. "Please sit in front, mademoiselle. Perhaps then you will learn to forgive me."

Phil climbed in back before his daughter could refuse Dragan's offer of reparations. He fingered the torn fabric of the backseat.

"Where do you get parts for this thing?"

"The car, you mean? I make them."

They drove around the footings of the Kalemegdan Castle. The sight of the trolleycars snaking their way under the broad plane trees filled him with strange joy. His wife had admitted —no, *announced*, admission was too tame—to engaging in an extramarital affair and he was watching how the generous early autumn sunlight filtered down to the street in its quiet, dusty, unhurried way. Was he in a state of dissociation, or had he developed philosophical distance? Or maybe become a Buddhist overnight as he slept, attaining the serenity of letting go, a perverse side effect of exposure to Bakelite? None of those things was like him, yet all could be true. By a streetcar stop, an ancient ruin of a car, a Zastava, the Yugoslavian equivalent of the East German Trabant, had been recycled into a storehouse for onions and garlic. That sight made him inexplicably happy. For once he did not question his happiness. In front, Dragan was busy repairing his mistake, or pretending to, putting on a tone more suitable to a daughter than a wife, but still gallant and attentive. Dana answered his questions playfully, unused to and enjoying the attention. The wind and street noise through the open window kept Phil from hearing the exact questions and answers. It was too bad because he was curious how Dana would represent herself to a stranger, a friend of her father. He did not strain forward to try and listen in. His daughter was conversing with his friend and liking it, and that was good enough.

Dragan's voice rose over the noise as they crossed the Pančevo Bridge.

"God has sent us these refugees," he told Phil. "Otherwise we would have fallen off the world map, completely, once again. As it is, the humanitarians have moved on to darker horizons. But with the refugees coming through... Look, even you're back!"

"Please, Dragan, I am not a humanitarian aid worker."

"I know. You are a news-hound. A news-monger. I love that word *monger*. But you represent renewed interest in our country. Admit it!"

"Yes. I admit. A magazine sent me. I guess that means you're right."

"We were the bad guys for a long time, and that made us interesting. But then we were forgotten. And now suddenly we are the good guys for being nice to refugees, and you can understand, we don't exactly know how to act." Dragan turned to look at Phil. The traffic ahead would look after itself. "But not such good guys. We gave the refugees Pančevo. It is one of the most polluted places in the region."

Inside the gym in the Pančevo school, three small boys were trying to put a basketball through a netless hoop. There was no hope they would succeed, ever. They were six or eight years old and the hoop was regulation height, they couldn't shoot the ball any more than half the elevation they needed, but every time they missed they laughed in outright pleasure, as if drunk on failure. The boys were deficient, held back in some way. Even an untrained eye could see that.

Dana stared at the game. It was hardly a game at all. It had an impossible goal and no rules.

"How can you look at that?" she asked her father. "Those kids are desperate."

"It's my job. And I think it's worthwhile for the world we live in to know what's going on in places like this."

"You get to say 'It's my job' only once. You just used it up."

"I don't know why, but somewhere along the way I developed an attachment to this place."

"He does not need to explain," Dragan told her. "It is his traumatic attachment!" How that expression ended up in his mouth was a mystery. "Come, we must find the central committee."

At the other end of the gym, a group of dark-eyed, sombre boys watched the would-be basketball players. They wanted their ball. They wanted to turn the basketball into a soccer ball. There were more of them, they were older and bigger, and they didn't appear to be victims of pollution, though in a state of shock, surely, which kept them from grabbing the ball and starting a different game with it. The local boys must have played soccer, everyone did. But the refugee kids didn't know how to negotiate, which was necessary if they wanted to begin a game. They had forgotten how to play.

Dragan watched the scene along with Phil and Dana.

"No international cooperation." He shook his head mournfully. "They are traumatized on both sides. That is to be expected. All of us are."

The central committee, as Dragan called it, had its headquarters in the foyer of the ruined school. An expertly made-up woman with a dazzling slash of lipstick drawn across her mouth was posted at a long table with stacks of papers set out in neat order, and bottles of water and wrapped sandwiches in a box at her feet. When she spotted Phil and Dragan, the woman rose from her classroom chair.

"I am Drinka. You have brought your interpreter. No need. We all speak English."

"He's my friend, not my interpreter."

Drinka looked dubious. In her experience, friendship between Westerners and Balkan people did not exist. There was always monetary exchange.

Phil turned to introduce Dana, but she was gone.

"I'll go make sure she's all right."

Discreet, Dragan stayed behind with Drinka as Phil went to the entrance to the gym. He looked in. The panels of windows around the top had been blown out. He hoped someone would put plastic over the gaping spaces before winter, then realized from the water damage on the floor that they had probably been like that for years.

Dana had gathered the three local boys around her. As they watched, she tentatively kicked their basketball toward the refugees. The ball was seriously underinflated, and the refugee side followed it as it wobbled across the floor toward them in a dubious trajectory. They might be refugees, but they were not very happy about playing with a ball like that. Then one of them took the hint. He stepped forward and kicked the ball to Dana. It was more of an acknowledgement than a real pass.

Dana stopped the ball and pushed it over to one of the local boys. Phil could not point to any one trait that made him think they were damaged in some way. They hadn't cared whether their ball made it anywhere near the hoop, and somehow to him, that stood for a loss of cause and effect, a game that had no goal, and only deficient children could enjoy it with such joy.

The local boy kicked the ball feebly in Dana's direction. She sent it back to him and pointed to the refugee kids who were watching intently. Her message got through. The boy struck the ball as hard as he could and it bounded toward the other group. He fell backward in the process, and both sides laughed at the recoil that was familiar to all of them. The game was on: the refugees vs. the forgotten children of the Pančevo ecological disaster delivered by NATO. That step forward in international relations was Dana's work. Phil couldn't remember her doing anything for anyone else since she was a child cutting out paper Valentines for her mother. It was time to widen the way he imagined her. He stepped out of the gym and went back to his work in a state of quiet elation.

Drinka and Dragan were drinking coffee served by a woman in a smock, an employee, though who employed her was not clear. Drinka looked up. A shadow of concern crossed her face.

"Sit," she said to Phil. "Have you seen a ghost?"

"No. I just saw something beautiful."

"I envy you. You are the only one to see such a thing here."

Drinka called for coffee for him. It was black and bitter, probably Nescafé assembled the day before, but it was the first step to creating community. He cut the coffee with sugar and was glad for the mineral water that rinsed the taste out of his mouth. Maybe a day would come when he would stop needing stimulants at regular intervals during the day, even if most of the world used them as well. In the middle of a piece on the refugee crisis in the Balkans, the urge to change his life was to be expected.

"Your friend Dragan tells me you have some experience in the region. That you are not one of those hit-and-run guys. That is a rare thing. But first you must tell me why you came to this place where no one, not even refugees, wants to stay any longer than necessary."

"Is it true that in that park in downtown Belgrade, the prostitutes put their money together to buy wire cutters for the refugees?"

"I have heard that story too. It warms my heart." She put her hand over her breast. "And who does not enjoy a story with sex in it? But maybe there is more to it. The women know that the refugee men will not be customers for them, and also they are scaring away the normal clients who might be afraid of refugees, so maybe this is their way to get them to move on, to Hungary, to Europe, to somewhere else."

"There are pimps for that."

"I am sorry, I do not know the word." She looked at Dragan. He shrugged. He knew the word, Phil suspected, but did not feel like explaining it to a proper humanitarian like Drinka.

"The men these women work for. They are their managers, you could say. Usually violent guys."

"I am sorry." Drinka shook her head. "We do not have such advanced social organization as you do in the West." She stood. "Now, come with me. It is time to test your pleasant assumptions about our big hearts."

The worst thing about being a refugee was the boredom—after the violence and insecurity, of course. In the former classrooms upstairs filled with foam mattresses with blankets piled on top, men were sitting, staring into space. There was almost no conversation. They had split into groups according to country, and then language and ethnicity. Periodically a man would shake himself from his torpor long enough to look at his phone's display. These machines were their lives, the wellspring of news, good and bad. With the border with Hungary closed, Drinka explained, an alternative had been found via Croatia. Unfortunately the alternative involved walking through fields and forests that had not been completely cleared of mines from the previous regional conflict. The Croatian government was warning refugees in English not to take that path, but not everyone understood, and many who did understand did not believe. The threat was just another way of closing the border and keeping them out. The classroom had only one wall socket, and the aid workers had laid out a power bar on the floor so that a half-dozen men could recharge their phones at once. The men were separated from the women, and the children assigned to the latter.

In the classroom that housed the women, the boredom was less oppressive. The women were putting their domestic skills to work. A number of them were embroidering ex-votos and commemorative depictions, scenes from the exodus that had taken them this far. Spontaneous art therapy was taking place. Maybe one day, in some northern European city, these women would have a show of their art in a fashionable gallery. Such things had happened before.

He moved closer to one of the embroiderers. She refused to look his way. Every woman's eyes were fastened on Dana. The women needed to be attentive to Drinka's expressions that were often hard to read for them. She was a source of their survival, untrustworthy because they depended on her, but necessary because she was helping them. Phil was a man with a notebook. They had had experience at every stop and every border with men like that, exploiters, story-stealers, salesmen out to sell them. But they had never seen anything like Dana, a girl healthy and free of constraint from some distant place, America, they figured, the only land where a woman could do what she wanted. She was a mythical creature, something out of the movies, the very thing the men in their countries warned them against becoming. They were burning to talk to her.

The embroidering woman set down her work and got painfully to her feet. She took Dana's hand.

Dana turned to Phil. "What do I do?"

"Get to know her. Start where you would with anyone else."

Dana kept the woman's hand in hers as she bent down to pick up the piece of embroidery. The woman was wrapped in blankets and scarves despite the warm autumn day and airless room, with the windows tightly shut as some sort of symbolic protection. Her clothes seemed to be keeping her from flying apart. Dana was young and beautiful and a good-luck charm for these women, and she had the advantage of wanting nothing from them. She could do my job better than me, Phil thought. He watched her intently. He had to remind himself that his daughter was not the reason he was here.

Dana held up the fabric. The work was clearly unfinished. It was hard to make out the image.

"What does it say?" she asked the woman in painstaking English.

Here was the history of every encounter between foreign tribes. They do not speak each other's language. A new language has to be invented, or someone found who can serve as a go-between, and who will not do too much damage by perverting the story.

The go-between was a young woman sitting nearby.

"I know what it says. I was there. She is making a picture because she cannot say what happened."

"Why not?"

"It did not happen to me, even if I am younger and some would say prettier. Though I do not think they consider prettiness. I smeared feces over my body and that was enough to make them not want me. I saved myself."

Dana looked at the cloth. The pattern on it looked nothing like what the go-between described. "Will she finish it?"

"It would be good if she did. But we don't know if she can."

157

Dana slowly understood what the young woman told her. "I could never do something like what you did."

The go-between shook her head. "Don't say that. You don't know what you could do. It would be better if you never have to find out."

Dana turned to the woman who had not smeared herself with shit and embraced her. Phil watched it happen. Maybe I won't get the story Susan wants, he thought, at least not here, not today. He was getting something better though.

He pictured Susan again on the sidewalk in front of the restaurant, brittle and successful and harried in that fairytale world. She was getting into a cab, her pleated skirt fluttering. She hardly existed anymore. She was as small as a pea, fading in his memory with every minute spent here. The woeful battle between him and Amy for the affection of their children that her affair, real or not, was part of—that was fading into insignificance too. The Balkans were magic. There was something in the water or the air that wiped away the petty and the small and everything non-elemental, and made it possible for a person to live without self-censorship. A romantic notion, certainly, but right then he was prepared to invest in it.

Back at the Palace, in the lobby Aperitiv Bar where they decompressed with Dragan at the end of the afternoon, Dana asked her father, "How are you supposed to react to stuff like that? I don't get how you do it."

"You write about it. Writing distances it."

"Do we want to get distanced?"

"Writing does that to any experience, especially the hardest kinds. All art does that. Think of the woman doing the embroidery. She was trying to do the same thing. It's something I like doing, no matter how hard it can be."

"Because it's supposed to be humanitarian?"

"Humanitarian is in far second place," Dragan broke in.

He was drinking a pear brandy, a double, with a mineral water chaser. Phil resisted, then settled for a beer. Of the three of them, Dragan was the most stressed. He had not been sent here by a glossy magazine of social inquiry and liberal good taste. This was his country. He would not be leaving when the job was done.

"Then what's in first place?" Dana asked him.

Dragan jerked his head in Phil's direction. "They are attracted to trauma, these people. They have strange attachments."

"Like me?"

"I don't know you well enough," Dragan said, suddenly guarded.

Phil had read her famine chronicles. He knew it was a family affair.

Dana turned to him.

"Are you attached to me the same way?"

"You are my daughter, and my love," he told her. "That is my attachment."

"Now you are on shifting sands," Dragan warned them. "As long as you know it, maybe it is all right." He finished his drink and called for another. "You will join me," he told Phil. "It is an obligation in this part of the world."

"If I must. But only if you stop playing the primitive."

"Ha! Very good! You know how to talk to people. It is a good example for your daughter. I have never heard of such a thing before: a man comes to work on a Balkan refugee story, in the Balkans, the place where we are producing more history than we can consume, and he brings his child with him. His daughter, a very pretty and intense mademoiselle. This is fantastic. It reminds me of a story I heard about an American soldier in Vietnam, a long time ago, back when the Americans put soldiers on the ground. He was lonely and afraid of death, so he sent for his girlfriend. Against all odds, she showed up in the middle of the jungle. In culottes—I don't know what that is. But it is not jungle wear, I know that much. Now, what you must understand," he said to Dana, "is that this man, your father, is respected by the people of this region. To hear a good story, you must be respected."

"Don't I get one?" Dana complained when the waiter brought the drinks.

"Women here don't drink this poison," Dragan told her, "unless they are menstruating."

Dana laughed loudly. "Don't worry, I'm not."

"Why would I worry?" Dragan pointed at her. "*Belo vino*."

The waiter reappeared instantly with a glass of white wine. He was a pro with the gift of anticipation, and he knew what ladies drank.

"All right, enough of family therapy," he said to Phil. "Were you satisfied with your day, considering it is only Day One?"

He was. Dana entered nearly every exchange at the Pančevo school, and every time something magical came of it. No, magical was a cheap word for what happened. Something unpredictable, *unheimlich*, untoward, exchanges he could not have imagined, nor initiated. Her naïveté was genius, unless it was not that at all, but a method of investigation. She did not see barriers where he felt them. People who were suffering opened up to her. He stood aside and took notes. There were hordes of journalists out there with the same assignment. None of them would get what he got. The rest of it—the non-intimate, the background info he would need to add to deliver an acceptable piece for Susan—he could pick that up from Drinka's organization and the dozens of other NGOs.

He raised his glass. "Nothing would have worked without Dana."

"I saw. It is a surprise effect. Like ambush."

"Have I become irreplaceable? That sounds a big responsibility."

"The cemetery is full of irreplaceable people. That is a saying we have. The world would continue to turn without you, but it would be a much poorer place."

Dana finished her wine and stood. "I am exhausted. This jetlag... Can I go?"

"Of course. Maybe we can have dinner... "

"Later," she said.

Dragan and her father watched her go up the dusty stairs. Every step was a mountain for her.

"Maybe I am being cruel," Phil speculated. "Too demanding."

"I could not say."

But Dragan *was* saying. It was fantastic for a man working on a story to bring his daughter with him to this part of the world. In the country Phil came from, Dragan speculated, there was probably a law against doing that. Phil had violated that law, and Dragan respected him all the more for it.

He rose smoothly to his feet, an experienced metabolizer of pear brandy. "Now it is my turn to go. My house. Back to reality."

"Don't try and pay," Phil warned him.

"If you can convince them to take your money, then you are a very persuasive man. You should go into politics instead." He pointed toward the ceiling, upstairs, to Dana's room. "She has something of the natural... How do you say, I am getting tired too. Whatever you call it. She has this ability. People talk to her."

"Women have that."

"Yes. And for your needs, women have the best stories, I think. Anyway, this gift she has… No doubt it carries a risk."

"It is born from pain," Phil assured him.

"Yes, I noticed. I saw something. You will forgive me for seeing."

On those words, they embraced, and promised each other more of the same tomorrow. Same time, same analytical hours.

Phil was enormously relieved to be alone in his room. That was the trouble with the job, the whole region. Both inspired hypervigilance. Everything was a story, everything was a clue, he tried to piece together the bit of the language he had learned and managed not to forget in order to figure out the mutterings of the hotel staff, who still did not believe Dana was his daughter. He tried to engage the barman in discussion about the piece he was writing, but the man suddenly lost his English at the mention of the word *refugee*. He was from Bosnia, and had had enough of the subject for several lifetimes. He waved off Phil's apology. "Bosnia is not your fault," he pointed out, then refused his money for the drinks with Dragan and Dana. "Later," the barman promised, "you will pay." But he could not stop Phil from leaving a tip on the table. That was his only victory over Balkan hospitality.

At the Pančevo school, in the foyer, he had tested out his theories on Drinka and the other women from her NGO, and they rejected them all. The citizens of Belgrade were more humane to refugees, he believed, because, in some way, they saw themselves as refugees too, and identified with them—that was his point of departure. Drinka and her sisters complimented him on his optimistic worldview, then replied with a catalogue of incidents of cruelty and violence inflicted by the police. The women returned over and over again to the word *humiliation*, a euphemism for sexual assault of one kind or another. Forty percent of refugees moving through their country were revictimized in some way or other, whether it was extortion, theft or anal rape, though as much violence came from other refugees as from their temporary hosts who saw a fleeting chance to take advantage of other human beings. "We are no more the country of the pure," Drinka insisted, "than we were the country of the evil in the last century."

Maybe they are comfortable only with a negative picture of themselves, Phil thought, at least in the eyes of the outside world. There were individuals like that. He had met a few. But could that be said of an entire country? While you're at it, you might as well assert that the French are romantic and the Germans rational and punctual. Welcome to the land of stereotypes where no worthwhile journalist goes.

But one thing did emerge, and it was verifiable, and made him happy, since it contradicted Susan's assumptions about ethnicity. There was no hostility based on religion. The citizens understood that these people moving through their country were Muslims who were not supposed to eat certain things, but the ones who brought them food were unclear about what was permitted or not. They argued among themselves futilely about dietary laws they knew nothing of. Pork, or no pork? Was beer alcohol? There were no imams to consult, only Google, and Google split into a plethora of interpretations. Pork was everywhere, and hard to avoid. Was it okay as long as it was well-cooked? Offer, the kind-hearted resolved, and let them decide. No one will curse us. Besides, if they have a God, then their God must be like ours: He loves His people more than He loves His laws, especially at a time like this.

Phil underlined those words in his notes. They carried wisdom for the ages, and from the ages. Once he vacationed on the north coast of the Dominican Republic, long before the tourism boom, a generation ago, when he and Amy had Dana, but not Megan, not yet, because they made her on that trip. Under the tropical sun he noticed several ancient Mitteleuropa types, stately men dressed in damp linen suits, out walking, obviously belonging to the place. He approached one of those men with his lizard skin and lizard-like wariness and got the story. He and his kind were refugees from Nazi Germany who had been dumped on the coast, since no other country in the free world would take them in. They married the women they came upon in this strange land, though they were not of the Hebrew faith, and the children who sprung from their loins would not be either. And though Phil said nothing, the man smiled at him unsteadily. "The Lord did not want us to sleep alone. He wished to reward our survival."

Drinka issued Phil a further caution. The locals could afford to be kind to refugees since they had no intention of staying. "It is one thing to have someone at your table for supper one night," she said. "Another to let him move into your house." With its twenty-five percent or higher unemployment and its language no one knew, with its history of instability, Serbia was hardly a beacon for anyone. The country produced immigrants. It did not take them in.

"What about all those Chinese I saw?"

"That is an anomaly. A Milošević idea. Actually, it was his wife who did that. A couple of harebrains. We will invite some Chinese to immigrate and they will vote for us. And they did. But now Milošević is just a bad memory, and we are stuck with a lot of lonely foreigners."

"Slovenia isn't a target for refugees," Phil countered, "but that country is doing all it can to keep them out. And what do the Hungarians think—that their nation is a magnet for Syrians and Afghans and Iraqis? It's just another stop on the way. But the Hungarians hung razor wire along their borders, which set off this whole mess in the first place."

"Slovenians think they are Germans, or Austrians at the very least," Drinka sniffed.

She had no similar national critique about Hungarians, but she did have her suspicions about Phil.

"Why are you so in love with us? This is not normal. You are supposed to be a Western journalist. You are supposed to be—how do you say it?"

"Impartial."

"Neutral. Something like that."

He shrugged.

"You must go to the border. You cannot be satisfied with just here," Drinka told him.

He had fared less well with the men in the upstairs rooms at the refugee school, and he knew why. That too would be part of his piece. In their home countries, the women lived on the receiving end of violence every day, but the men were used to being hammers, not nails. They walled themselves off in their unaccustomed victim status. They could not protect their women, and they could hardly protect themselves. In the past, many had fought and been captured and experienced legendary cruelty, but that was war, that was to be expected. But they were not soldiers anymore, they had deserted hopeless fights in unlivable countries, and now they had no status, no power, no brotherhood, no purpose outside of this endless forward plodding surrounded by strangers.

Dana did not go into the rooms where the men were lodged. She was afraid, and so was Phil, for her. Her magic would not have worked. Dana met her point of resistance there, at that doorway upstairs. Pančevo was Dragan's idea. Shock therapy, start with the worst first. Tomorrow was downtown Belgrade and the camp in the park. The atmosphere had to be better. It could hardly be worse than the Pančevo chemical dump.

Though Susan hadn't mentioned it in so many words, she placed an unspoken demand on him, something he must include in his piece, since the readers of her magazine would look for it first thing: the differences between the women and the men who were part of this exodus. Like all humanitarians, her readers were avid consumers of the pornography of violence. Well, he had one story for them already, and it was terrifying. But one would probably not be enough for their appetite. What could he do—there were so few women on this journey. It was the pattern of immigration. When Phil's ancestor set out for America without a mobile phone and a GPS, it was the same. The men left and sent for the women when they could. Or didn't send for them. They started new lives. They tore down, then built up; they became new men. At first Phil felt great sadness when he thought of those women left behind, and was surprised to learn that many of them were just as happy that way.

There was another vulnerable group he had not considered, and was discovering, and those were teenage boys, some so young they had hardly begun puberty, which often was delayed by the trauma of their trip. Violence exploded among these boys when they were thrown together in camps by governments that did not know what to do with them. The camp was a trusty European model, but it produced cruelty that came straight out of *Lord of the Flies*, or worse. The only way to protect the youngest and the weakest of the boys was to keep them out of camps.

With all these demoralizing prospects, in a hotel room so narrow he could put his palms on both walls at once, Amy intruded into his thoughts. Not Amy the person—the atmosphere of Amy, the attitude of her body. The way lately, and no doubt it was more than just lately, she showed her body to him with such disinterest. A lover will drape her body and cover it in disguises and veils until the moment she chooses to let the fabric fall. Amy had taken to marching out of the bathroom and into their bedroom naked as if to prove her point about having a body of no further interest. An old cloak you let slip off the back of a chair and onto the floor with no further regard, a garment no longer in fashion.

A life without a woman's desiring, he thought mournfully, was a life not worth living. Then he scolded himself for being melodramatic, not surprising given his situation, far from home, under pressure, the prey of multiple stressors beginning with duty-free Calvados that can lead to easy sentimentality. The thought of Lynne and her studied neutrality intruded on him, the dispiriting way she allowed him to hold her until he gave up. That was harder to live with than adultery, a word that did not belong in this century. His wife had a lover, or so she said. Well, he had too, in the past. He had kept those occurrences to himself during the short period the affairs raged. That had not been hard to do in his compartmentalized life. And he had certainly not taken out the emotional remote control and programmed his child to report on his fleeting love interest to his wife. He had not done everything, in word and in deed, to de-eroticize his marriage.

The four scans Amy sent him lay closed on the desktop. He

looked over at the computer with its dull single winking eye indicating it was ever-watchful, ready to spring from sleep at a single touch. You may be, he addressed the machine, but I am not. There was no good way to answer her message. He literally did not have the words. What a man cannot speak of, he must pass over in silence—his favourite philosopher said that.

The bushes in the Park of the Ministry of Finance were being used to dry laundry. Clothing and headscarves were carefully laid across the shrubs and knotted to the branches so the wind would not cast them back onto the ground where seventy-five refugees sat on flattened cardboard boxes, awaiting their next move. They had not travelled with the tubs they used to do their laundry. The locals supplied them.

"Take some pictures of washday," Phil told Dana. "I'll make sure you get credit and get paid."

"We don't know about the wire-cutters," Dragan said. "But the pails for washing, and the soap, yes. And the water from the fountains. So those are points for us as good guys."

"It's good for the story."

"Yes, but not so interesting. There is no sex in pails."

The park was officially named for the ministry that stood across the wide, sunny expanse of lawn. It was a logical spot for a camp, with the bus and train stations just down the slope of a hill, close to the river. The local men called it Pussy Park in honour of the women who worked the spot in the evening. A chic restaurant owned by a former basketball star stood at one edge of the park, and the waiters brought out leftover food at the end of the evening. The refugee social networks must have spoken of that feature of the stopover. Beyond the restaurant stood the hulking ruins of government buildings bombed by

NATO. If you were a Belgrade citizen, you necessarily got used to those monuments and stopped seeing them, but Phil felt them glaring down at him, late-twentieth-century remnants of what warfare had become, with all the courage needed to attack from thirty thousand feet. He hoped their social networks would explain the origin of the ruins so the travellers' morale would not be worsened as they waited in the park for something to happen.

Beyond the washtubs and laundry soap and leftover restaurant food, these people received the gift of respect. Belgrade citizens came down to look at them, and see whether they resembled the pictures on TV. They did not. The images from the border between Macedonia and Greece had shown chaos and crying women and shell-shocked children and grim men. Here in the park, the women were industriously washing clothes while the men stared at their mobile phones, something people did all over the world. The few children who were part of the voyage slept. No one harassed them, not even drunk teenagers at night. The police kept their distance, and the ladies who came to offer food were so shy it was painful for both sides.

Along with the waiters and housewives, there were endless visits from professionals, local NGOs, doctors, and refugee specialists who were part of the region's enormous expertise that had accumulated over recent decades. Those people were part of Phil's story too. Here, unlike Pančevo, the story was writing itself along ideal lines. He was afraid of turning into an advocacy journalist who did not investigate the truth, but only sought proof of his opinion.

"There's something festive about this place."

"Festive?" No matter how much American TV Dragan watched, there were words that eluded him.

169

"Like a rock concert or something."

"Ha! Woodstock in Belgrade, only with Afghan refugees and no music. You have the gift of imagination. And this is not only a compliment."

It was less-than-perfect journalism, but Phil had to depend on the refugees who knew some English, and those were the younger, better-educated ones. They all claimed to be engineers, chemical, electrical or mechanical or all three, and they looked the part, serious and remarkably clean considering what they had gone through to get this far, which was still several borders from their goal. The dignity of keeping clean must play some part in survival. In every case, he felt the person he talked to was holding something back. Not lying outright, but keeping sections of his experience concealed. That was to be expected, and made the woman who told Dana how she foiled the rapists all the more extraordinary. Maybe she repeated the story to all who would hear it, hoping to expel it from her body like a poison. It was like vomiting, Phil thought, only over and over again.

He took out his notebook and balanced it on his knee. *These are the kind of people any country should be happy to have*, he wrote. Then he crossed out *happy* and put *grateful* in its place. Qualified and enormously determined. People unafraid to walk through walls to reach a better life, or any life at all. People who just wanted to be part of the world. Immigration is wealth. He wondered how his readers would take to that statement. They came from somewhere else too, but many had forgotten that fact.

He shared the thought with Dragan.

"So many engineers, it is like a plague. Be careful, those people are good at making bombs. Not that I am worried. They will not use their skills here. We have become one of the most secure spots on the globe."

Phil shook his head. "I only wish I had your cynicism."

"I am the ideal fixer. Not only do I drive you where you want to go, I curb your enthusiasm. I am your *repoussoir*."

"That's what they call a friend, I believe."

They watched Dana move idly through the crowd, without connecting to anyone, getting no closer to people than what it took to ask them permission for a photo.

"She is tired from yesterday, perhaps. Who can keep up this intensity? It requires the training you have."

"She's looking. She'll find someone. A woman."

"No doubt, with her gift, she will succeed. You will forgive me," Dragan ventured, "but what inspiration came over you to bring this child here?"

"I wanted her to get out of herself. Back home, most of the time she lives in her room."

"And you didn't want to be alone," Dragan presumed.

"Yes. It's a relief to have her here, even if yesterday she went upstairs and stayed there. I know she's near. And I have the feeling this will be my last big trip. The journalism business is falling apart. I haven't worked much recently."

"At least they are not killing you."

"No. They're killing us with indifference. The unkindest way."

"The advanced, Western way. So you need to find a way to make yourself indispensable. We will go to the border zones. There, with a little luck, we will see things that will make your readers sick with guilt. That way, they will hire you again and again."

"Here's hoping!"

Dana came up and stood by their side. "I'm just staring at people. It's like the zoo. I don't feel comfortable. Prospecting for human misery isn't right if you ask me."

"You didn't feel that yesterday."

"That was different. The woman came to me. She had that cloth. Here I have no way in."

"Then it is time for lunch," Dragan decreed.

The convenient thing about covering the Balkans is that everything is so close by, which accounts for the production of so much history on such a small territory. The Hungarian border crisis had been well reported on, but the new front opening up along the line separating Serbia from Croatia had no one on it as far as Phil knew, and Dragan had not heard of any foreign journalists heading in that direction. "Nobody but the humanitarians are there now," he said, "your new best friends." It was an hour's ride to Šid, the nearest town to the crossing and the logical staging point for refugees trying to make it into the European Union's newest member state.

"It's an easy day's trip," Dragan explained. "Just as well since there's really nowhere to stay out there."

"We could sleep outside, like they do," Dana said. "That way you'd have a better idea of how they live."

"That's called identification journalism," Phil answered, "where you pretend to be at one with your subject. I don't believe in that. There are a hundred reasons why that's wrong. Starting with the fact that we're not refugees."

"And we are too old to sleep outside, on the ground," Dragan added.

Dana did not care much for her father's professional scruples. The essential act was to identify with people, and take on their pain. That's what it meant to be human. Describing the refugee crisis as a footrace between journalists or a pleasure excursion offended her, and so did Dragan's cavalier attitude toward the human tragedy that was starting to overwhelm her. She stared out the car window at the highway. A go-kart track, incongruous in this place, sat unused in the bright sunlight. World War II-era tractors, everything vintage in this place, were busy in the fields on both sides of the road, harvesting whatever people ate here, mostly red peppers and grilled meat as far as she could tell. The tractors sent up plumes of black diesel exhaust into the air. Everywhere was the fullness of warm, fertile autumn, but it did not move her. The Balkan plain was unendingly generous. You could drive a dry stick into the earth and it would turn into a fruit tree, or so went the peasant proverb. That meant nothing to Dana. She absorbed the tensions of the place, but was immune to its mad joy. She waited for the interruption of atrocity. The woman who had smeared feces on her body sat next to her, still unwashed, on the backseat.

After a time, Dana closed her eyes. A minute later, the picture of that woman jerked her from her shallow sleep. Her father was gazing at her.

"Sleep, Dana. You need it."

"I can't."

And she told him how there was no sleep in her room at the Palace, not a minute of it. "The bed is worse than the cots at that summer camp you made me go to one year."

"I don't remember that," Phil admitted. "Have you tried reading? You brought all your files."

"I did. But it's not working. I read over all that stuff I have with me, and it doesn't mean anything to me anymore. I don't understand. And then…"

She stopped. Phil did not urge her to go on. He could imagine her regret when she said the word *affair*, and saw the look on his face.

173

The car rocked and bounced over rough ground and her head flew back against the padded headrest. She was awake.

"You slept an hour. That's good."

She didn't know if that was good or not.

"You must have needed to."

She looked out the window. *Vintage* meant something dif-ferent here. It was not about Bakelite telephones that could be polished and sold in shops. It meant abandonment, not recycling or finding new uses with kitschy undertones. Here it looked like they just walked away from their houses and villages and left them to collapse, untended.

Dragan drove into a vacant lot. Phil recognized two white Jeeps from the UN High Commission for Refugees.

"The Opeska Brickyard," Dragan explained. The tour guide's ironic gallantry was gone. "Mortar attack in 1992, hasn't been used since. Until now. Now it's full of people."

"How far are we from the border?"

"A few kilometres at most."

They stepped out of the car into the swirling pink dust of thousands of pulverized bricks. Behind the building, railroad tracks led west, toward the refugees' destination. The tracks were their drinking gourd. No freight had travelled on them since the last regional conflict, decades ago.

They walked around the edge of the building, Dana trail-ing. The west-facing side was blown out, and on the loading dock above the tracks, men sat slumped against the one outside wall that was still intact, wrapped in blankets in the mellow Sep-tember air. Some men stared into the distance. Others slept in the sitting position. The exhaustion and discouragement and determination were palpable.

They walked through the gaping wall into an inner court-yard.

"Is this place safe?"

"Safe?" Dragan echoed. He looked at the ground at his feet. "The site was never mined, just shelled, and only once as far as I know. With a little luck there's no unexploded ordnance. So many people have been through here since the war, they would have hit it before us. So, safe." He smiled and spoke his favourite English phrase. "We are on the safe side."

Inside the courtyard, there were a half-dozen fires going, made from splintered wood beams and planks. The people were warming themselves in the mild autumn air, terminally and forever cold from their journey.

"How did they find this place? It can't be on anyone's GPS."

"You'd be surprised." Dragan pointed out the aid workers in their UN jackets. "We will ask them. It is better protocol."

It turned out the refugees did not find this place. They were brought here after being beaten back at the border with Croatia. There they tried a tactic that had worked elsewhere: the human wave. They moved forward, impassive and disobedient, expecting to overwhelm the border guards and push down the interlocking steel fences. But for a wave to work, you need numbers, and they were not numerous enough. When they surged forward, the border guards pepper-sprayed them in the face and beat them with nightsticks. Some made it through, a few always do, but they were picked up by the police several kilometres into Croatian territory. Before they dumped them back on the Serbian side, the cops smashed their mobile phones. Everyone in the brickyard was a member of that unsuccessful wave. They first gathered in the town of Šid, in Serbia, where the good citizens did not want them in the centre where there was a transit post, a remnant of the civil wars, with running water and cots and a functional roof. The villagers launched rumours of an axe attack at a farmhouse by an unknown, unidentified, brown-skinned refugee, and the mayor informed the Belgrade government that he could not guarantee the refugees' safety for more than the next twelve hours. The Belgrade office of the UNHCR was contacted and they transferred them out of the town to the brickyard.

"So they will wait," Phil said, "and try again."

"Well, there is nothing to go back to."

"Sooner or later they will succeed."

"We see this phenomenon elsewhere in nature."

The UNHCR workers moved among the people, checking on their wounds. Most seemed superficial. The worst loss, and the police knew it, was the mobile phones. Cut off from their social networks, the refugees were at the mercy of whoever would give them information, true or false, and more vulnerable to the smugglers, most from their home countries, who promised to get them into "the game," as they called it. Closed borders let the profiteers prosper. They took a deposit of a thousand dollars from the refugees and made them sign a contract: they would receive the deposit, less fees, once they made it to the other side.

"I'd like to talk to the smugglers."

"They would not like to talk to you. What would they say? That they are doing this for humanitarian reasons? There are probably smugglers right here in this building, but we cannot recognize them. Some of them are refugees too. This is their way of working their way north. But they are refugees without solidarity."

A second camp, the UN workers told them, had been set up in a motel off the highway. It was their next destination. Phil and Dragan stepped out of the courtyard and saw Dana standing on the abandoned railroad track, looking west, toward Croatia, the beginnings of Europe.

"I could walk that way and get to the border, right?" she asked. "It wouldn't take long. Then what would happen?"

"You'd cross over if you had your passport," Phil said. "It is a good one to have."

"You always told me to keep it with me."

"Then you're in."

"That's not fair."

"It's an accident of birth. Don't blame yourself."

She squinted into the western light. "I want to try it. One day I will. I swear I will."

Dragan pointed to the UNHCR workers conferring in the dusty pink parking lot.

"You could do what they do. Their job."

"I don't know their language."

"Anyone can learn it. Even your father did, partway. If you want to speak to people anywhere in the world, learn an immigrant language."

The ride to the motel took five minutes. It lay just off the Highway of Brotherhood and Unity that was now called the E-70. Though it had not been hit by mortar shells, it too was a casualty of past conflicts. No one travelled much on the highway between Zagreb and Belgrade, and those who did didn't want to stop along the way among bad memories, or worse.

Two white UN Jeeps were parked outside the Auto-Motel, closed for lack of guests. Dragan stood by the front of the car and stared at the low building, his face transformed. This was not what Phil was expecting.

"I know this place. I used to take a girl here, I remember. A woman. She was married. Fifteen years older than me. I was only nineteen, just a kid. It was heaven, I'm telling you. She made me what I am, the better part of me that is left. If it is not all gone. I think that was the last time I did good for a woman. She had a joke she used to say, I still remember, in bed, she was so sweet with me. She would tell me, 'I am…'" He grasped for the words. He turned to his mobile phone, typed away furiously, then smiled with great satisfaction. "'I am insatiable, and you are indefatigable.'" He looked up at Phil. "Are those really words?"

"At the best of times. And now you are visiting her again."

"I should tell her I am here… if I could find her. Only God knows where she is."

He crossed himself, love and superstition. Then they went into the motel through the reception where UN aid workers were busy on their mobiles. Dragan pointed to one of them.

"She is Croatian, that one, talking to her colleagues in Zagreb. If you are looking for good news from the Balkans, she is for you. Former enemies are cooperating for the sake of refugees."

There was very little additional good news in the motel rooms. The people had travelled from the closed Hungarian border where their wave had been stopped with razor wire and attack dogs whipped on by soldiers. Some boys, teenagers at most, had their hands and arms bandaged from dogbites. Phil tried to imagine himself at sixteen, having walked halfway around the world to come up against a razor-wire fence, and be set on by German shepherds. What was the worst that had happened to him? Bad mescaline and a case of crab lice. These people were beyond what Phil thought of as determination. They would spend the rest of their lives dealing with the damage from the places they left and the journey they made, if ever they reached their destination. He knew his readers associated the word "refugee" with Syria, but as far as he could tell, most of these people started out in Afghanistan. Added to them was a mix of people from every other refugee-producing country in Asia and Africa. He did not see a single woman or child.

Phil and Dragan went from room to room, talking to whomever would talk to them. Dana followed, studying the UN workers. In one room they were passing out fruit from the orchard on the other side of the road. The men, a couple dozen per room, were munching on pears. An aid worker gave Dana one. It was enormous. She slipped into the bathroom between the men waiting for a shower and went to the sink to wash it.

"You think we would give people unwashed fruit, with all the pesticides still on it? We are not uncivilized, you know."

The aid worker laughed, all white teeth and red lipstick.

"It was here. Right here," Dragan said. "This is the room."

"You always went to the same room?" Phil asked.

"She wanted it that way. It was our lucky room. We were happy here. She was superstitious when it came to happiness. She did not have much of it—her words, not mine." Dragan stepped forward and touched the bed covered with sleeping refugees. "This is the bed."

Phil looked at the chaos of wounded men covered in blankets with their packs scattered on the floor. "How can you tell?"

"The picture." He pointed at a generic sunset painting. "She would sleep afterwards, not me. With us it was the opposite of how it is with men and women. She needed to sleep. I would hold her and look at the picture."

Phil went over to it. Dragan should have this painting, a mass-produced reproduction, beyond ugly. But it was nailed to the wall.

"I'm sorry."

"No matter. How would I explain to my wife? I go to see refugees and come back with an ugly painting. And where would I put it?"

Dragan laughed. They were miles off-topic, but Phil loved this story. Somehow it was part of the global refugee crisis too. It was one of those things that happen when you walk out into the world, with everything falling away behind you, including the place you once lived in.

That evening, exhausted and undecompressed even after decompressing at the Aperitiv Bar with Dana and Dragan, Phil went over his notes to save the shock of first impressions. On some pages he could hardly read what he had written, and he was afraid of losing some telling detail through forgetfulness. During one of their first sessions, he had worried with Dr. Sheridan whether he might have forgotten some crucial point or other. *It is impossible that you forgot,* she told him. *It is in you somewhere. It will return.* Her optimism gave him no comfort. The note-taking conditions were difficult. Often he had his notebook propped on the edge of a chair or on the dashboard of Dragan's car. He recorded Dana's comments along with everything else, and they were mixed in with the refugee accounts and the UN worker's appeal to the West made through him, the woman who had given his daughter a washed pear. One man at the motel would not accept the pear. He would not hold it in his hand. Through their stumbling collective English, his brothers explained that it looked like a grenade to him. That might bring an indulgent smile or an expression of pity from Phil's readers, but not from him. He looked closely at the pear and saw it could be a grenade. The stem was the pin. All fruit could look like a grenade. He made a note of that too.

Phil knew that the various Balkan factions in his audience would follow every word when his piece came out, and imagine messages and conspiracies between the lines. He did not want to be accused of being pro-Serbian again. What he learned today would help him avoid the charge, and tread the middle ground. The Serbian mayor of Šid was a run-of-the-mill fear-mongering racist, while the Croatian aid worker had come from her country equipped with a Croatian phone and a Serbian phone to coordinate with her colleagues on both sides of the border. If anything, he was pro-refugee, but that was no problem. Everyone who read Susan's magazine was, at least until those people started moving into their neighbourhoods.

Being bone-tired did not protect Phil from a feverish state of hyper-arousal. This assignment connected him with his inner refugee, starting with his grandfather, a man he had never known, who'd made a journey somewhat like this, but without a shred of technology. That was part of his piece, the backstory: what he owed that generation. He would figure out a way to get that into the text when he started writing. Thanks to his grandfather, through him, he was born and lived and did a job that meant moving backward through space to this demanding region that so many had fled. Maybe he could do some good for these refugees, someone's future grandfather who would keep his ordeal hidden in silence the way his grandfather must have done.

And the refugees were providing him a service. They kept his wife's message far from his mind during the day, and on into the evening, when finally the effect of his work wore off and he could not avoid her anymore. He awoke the computer and clicked on the first scan. Now what? Literary analysis? Reading between the lines like his conspiracy-minded audience back home? Noting her lack of emotion, as if she owed him a glorious confession of her feelings for another man? Don't interpret. Better yet, don't read. Who cares if it's denial—it's better for your health.

No. It is not denial. It is avoidance. There must be a difference.

And I have other things to do. I don't owe her an answer. She didn't ask for one. Some information does not require immediate action.

But the temptation was too great. He was a reader. So he read. That's what he did for a living, at least some of the time. And when he did read her, he understood Amy could not make a confession without bringing him in for some share of blame. He wondered if she did that when she was young and went to church. *It's your fault if I sinned.* How would that have gone over in the confessional?

His fault was obvious. He was a partner and co-creator of a marriage. Marriage was dreary and possessed of sameness. An affair was exciting, the antidote to marriage. Amy made her affair sound like marriage. He could have suspected her of trying to spare him, but she had never done that before.

He jumped over to his online dictionary and looked up the word *placate*. Appease, pacify. She had never undertaken either of those actions since he'd known her. Whoever the man was, the co-creator of the affair, he did not know her very well. His pleasure might lay in that fact.

Phil pictured the dresses and sweaters he had bought her over the years that never came out of the closet, that she wore once and hung on a hanger, though they still looked good on her, at least in his eyes. Finally she was putting those gifts to use. The same went for the blank book. He bought her a diary and she turned the convention inside out. He did not have to pick the lock to discover the truth. She exposed it willingly, if not happily.

He looked around the hotel room. A few days into the trip, it appeared exactly what it was: dismal, fusty, a relic from the days of Tito. He did not want to go home. Nothing with Amy was real as long as he stayed away. He could be a refugee.

He could start a new category, emotional refugee, a refugee from marriage, fleeing an unlivable situation like real refugees, but unlike them, without a destination, on the move, always moving. He could be one of those people he disapproved of, and imitate the object of his research. But there was no reality to that plan, not with Dana in his life. Good thing she was here. If he attempted something like that, she would see through his disarray, and he believed that children should not have to mother their parents. As it was, he felt her grasping for a way to go back on the words she had blurted out.

The night ended without any answer for Amy. He imagined her relief. He clicked the scans shut, and they followed him into his sleep.

Part of the job, Phil told Dana over breakfast the next morning, was doing nothing and letting the place come to them. The last few days had been spent in frenetic activity, the rush from one disaster scene to the next as Dragan or the UN workers called the play-by-play. But if you wanted to succeed in the portrait of a place, you had to sit quietly and do nothing.

That afternoon, Phil and Dana went out in search of the ideal sidewalk café. They chose a makeshift installation composed of two metal tables with umbrellas over them, sheltered in turn by the great plane trees, and completed by a closed-face matron who looked as though she hadn't smiled in a generation. Phil ordered white wine and an equal volume of mineral water. Dragan was killing him with his pear brandy. It was the afternoon, a time for something milder and more convivial. He was tired of damaging himself with the local spirits.

The matron poured them a glass of wine and a glass of water from the two carafes, and called Dana "Madame." The country was determined to marry them.

Dana took a sip of wine and made a face.

"Cut it with water," Phil suggested. "That's how it works."

"A spritzer, how sophisticated." She filled the space in her wine glass with mineral water. "I suppose you were hard at work last night."

"I looked at my notes."

"Did the WIFI work for you?"

"On and off. You have to be patient. And not very ambitious about the sites you're trying to look at."

"I looked up 'Having an Affair.'"

"How many results did you get? Quite a few, I imagine."

Dana took another long swallow. She was determined to triumph over her inhibitions and say whatever was on her mind. Go ahead, daughter, Phil thought, this is the time.

"I don't feel so bad. I mean, about you and Mom. That's the main thing."

"I'm glad for you. Can I ask why?"

"Well, it's weird. On one hand an affair is this thing that's supposed to be so bad because you have to keep it secret, but on the other hand everyone does it. So I don't get it."

Phil smiled. It was worth having children for a conversation like this. He felt bad for men who stayed childless. Most of all, it was worth having a girl like Dana who was slightly off topic, off-centre. A young woman who accepted the conventions of sex would not think this way, and say these things. An affair, after all, is about conventions. Sex, in almost every case, except the most passionate, is about conventions too.

"But I don't get that Mom did it. I mean, she's too... How old is she? I can't see it, I mean, not according to the stuff I read."

"Children can't picture their parents having a sex life. That's the way it's supposed to be. And you know that not everything on the net..."

"Not everything online is true. Don't worry, Dad, I know that."

"And you also know that people my age are not the number one market of web sites like the ones you looked at. And since we're on the subject of what's true, and less true, we also have to consider that what your mother said might not be true."

Dana was completely shocked. "How can you say that?" The possibility entered her, little by little. "If that's true, then it's worse than having an affair."

"You're right, in a way. But let's be generous to her. Maybe she was just trying to send us a message—I mean, *me* a message. Sometimes people say something partly true, or that could be true, but that isn't, not completely, in order to get our attention."

Dana slumped back in her metal chair. It scraped against the concrete sidewalk. Phil had gone too far and gotten too labyrinthine, and that was a form of parental cruelty. Dana was clearly not equipped to handle affairs, symbolic or not. Megan was younger, but she would have done a lot better with the subject, which is why Amy had chosen Dana to carry the mail. Sex and lots of it was Megan's protection against her sister's disorders, her war on becoming a woman. As long as Megan had boyfriends, stacks of them, she would never turn into her sister. Those boys would never know they owed their incredible good luck to their lover's disturbed sibling.

"What are you going to do now? Break up with Mom? Don't you have to?"

"Is that what you read on the net?"

"Not exactly. Sometimes. On the other hand they said an affair can strengthen a marriage. Though I don't get how that would work. I mean… Forget it."

"I suppose the net was trying to say that an event like that can wake people up to each other and get them talking again."

He raised his glass in Dana's direction. She cut him off before he could propose a toast.

"Are you going to do that? Are you going to start talking to her?"

Phil saw how much it truly mattered to her. Unfortunately, he was committed to the truth. "I'm not sure. Right now I can't think of a single word to say to her."

"Your feelings are hurt."

She shook her head sadly. Phil felt like crying. Her sadness, and his too, and their wonderful new bond together. To keep from crying, he talked.

"Let's drink to our trip together. It certainly has been busy. We deserve some time off. A toast to this moment. There should be more of them."

They clinked their glasses, which produced a dull, stony sound. The proprietress of the installation allowed herself a half smile. It was a historical moment.

"When you get back home, if you like, you can talk with your mother. You know, woman to woman."

"I certainly would never do that." Dana would not poke around in her mother's sexuality because, with her child's logic, such a thing could not exist. Then she came up with another unexpected solution. "I'd rather have an affair myself. Is that possible, or do I have to be married?"

"You can have a torrid affair if you like. All you need is the right person to feel torrid about."

"Wait a minute—you went on those same sites! The word 'torrid' comes up everywhere."

"It's a cliché, trust me."

"And I suppose you think clichés are automatically bad?"

"Okay, not a cliché. A thing people like to say."

They eased into the afternoon, carried along by sour white wine made palatable by good-quality mineral water. A man approached them and tried to sell them a broom. When Phil waved him off, he offered two brooms. Another wandered by in search of wicker chairs to re-cane, but their sidewalk café had only metal ones. A team of teenagers swarmed past them, halted in the middle of the street, laid down a stencil and spray-painted a logo on the pavement. Twenty or thirty years ago, it would have been a call to oppose the regime. *Gotov je* —he's finished—and a picture of Milošević. Phil had plenty of relics from the campaign against the dictator, all the *Otpor* T-shirts he took out of a drawer and wore when he pitched a story to advertise the boldness of his past career. But today the street was advertising the opening of a new nightclub. At one point Phil stole a look at Dana. His daughter was asleep in her chair. Had the mix of wine and whatever she was taking for her moods felled her? More likely the affair exhausted her, the ins and outs of strange adult conflict. He couldn't blame her. How had Amy, his faithless wife, described it? *The weight, the bother and effort of it, the repetition.* Her real infidelity was against the affair itself. If he was going to have a revenge affair, and all the websites discussed that dishonorable motivation, he would do better than *bother* and *effort*.

Then he understood. The words described their marriage. As for the affair, she had to be enjoying it richly. She said so herself: it had become her primary relationship.

The next day Phil was back on the road, this time without Dana. He and Dragan drove out to Šid again. The brickyard had been emptied out, and its population replaced by the next wave.

187

These people could not be stopped. The scale was biblical. Phil made a note to reread the Exodus story. What happened once the miracles did their work and Moses and the children passed through the Red Sea dry-shod? He wasn't sure. Something told him they kept wandering. Moses never crossed over to the Promised Land. He would need to look that up. He could use it in the piece, but he had better be careful. It was amazing the things he half-knew, and he could imagine the mess that would ensue if he got one of the world's greatest stories wrong.

Without Dana, the pace was faster and more strenuous, much to Dragan's approval. They followed the new group from the brickyard who were setting out through the fields toward the border on a tractor path. They angled northwest out of Šid, away from the crossing that was most closely guarded. Phil got what he was hoping for, the coordination between the UNHCR in Serbia and their counterparts in Croatia. Both were at war with the Croatian border guards, though once not long ago they had been at war with each other. At first Phil was tempted to call the procedure a game, since the guards did let a certain number of people through at certain times, and no doubt they knew that sooner or later everyone would find a way in. Their tactic was to torture people with uncertainty. That had worked before. The philosopher Walter Benjamin killed himself rather than face the doubt of being handed back to the French authorities after he had crossed illegally into Spain during World War II. But the attack dogs and clubs and pepper-spray kept Phil from writing the word *game*. And it had the wrong association. Smugglers used it in their dealings with their victims.

At one point along the path a man, Afghan or Pakistani, veered off and started to head into the fields, lowering his zipper to take a pee. A Serbian aid worker, a woman, grabbed him by the shoulder and pulled him back onto the centre of the track. The man was mortified. A woman had touched him, she grabbed him, she kept him from urinating. The terrible things that happened to refugees, the humiliation! The couple dozen men in the group stopped to watch the event. The woman explained but the man knew no English, or was too mortified to understand, and the others were of no help because they did not want to participate in the man's humiliation. The word for landmine was the same in Serbian and English and French and every other European language, but the man who wanted to pee was too shocked to process the information that saved his life. The woman had to execute an eloquent charade to get the point through to him.

Then came a line in the fields that only the aid workers knew was there. It was the border to Croatia, and Europe. From out of a shed that held farm tools, a group of aid workers appeared in their bright vests. They were not trying to hide. Their job was to be as visible as possible. Phil stopped and stood with Dragan and watched the men go carefully down the centre of the path. *"Bon voyage!"* Dragan called. Then they were gone behind a line of trees that put them out of sight. So much effort for something seemingly so uneventful. There would be people who would want to hunt them down and kill them, and others who would give them safe haven. In the best cases there would be follow-ups with doctors and interviews with interpreters and beds in barracks and the quest for work and something close to dignity. Some of them would wish they had stayed home and others would explode with hatred for their new surroundings. Probably at least one of them would write a book about what happened. But no one could be absolutely sure of what would become of each of them in the future.

Two days later, Dragan took Phil and Dana to the airport, a humble terminal that hardly seemed up to international standards in the midst of a freshly harvested cabbage field. The atmosphere was relaxed. There were no guards carrying machine guns like in Paris. A few cab drivers were soaping down their cars in the taxi pool while another phalanx waited in the shade of some scrubby trees, stoking a cooking fire underneath shish kabob skewers.

The three got out and stood in front of the PT Cruiser.

"We must devise a plan," Dragan announced, "to help us cope with our separation anxieties."

"Always the psychiatrist. Tell you what. When this story is published I'll come back and put a copy in your hand. It will be a solemn occasion."

"Then maybe we will have some enjoyment instead of working all the time."

"I took an afternoon off with my daughter," Phil defended himself.

"You need to chase women," Dragan decreed. "You are not a typical man. What is wrong with you?"

"Time spent with you is more valuable," Phil countered.

"He needs to have an affair," Dana said.

"No doubt, but he must not admit to it. That makes a terrible mess." Dragan shook his head with profound sadness. "Marriage is unsolvable."

He embraced Phil, then Dana, circumspectly. "Since you are coming back soon, we do not have to feel as sad as we normally should. What do you say to that?"

Phil dreaded the reunion at the airport, with Amy executing her conjugal duty by picking up Dana and him. He spent the flight back from Paris thinking of what to say to her, and finding nothing, and concluding again that there was nothing he could say. From the Roissy airport he texted her not to come, and she answered swiftly, as if she had been waiting: *Nonsense. I'll be there.* From across the aisle, Dana was looking at him with something very much like compassion. He had never seen that on her face. He smiled at her, and felt the labour of executing that smile. Be like her, he resolved. Be like Dana. Use her off-centre wisdom and defeat the conventions that dictate how you're supposed to act. And somehow, magically, you will be all right. If there was ever a time for magical thinking, it was now.

Then he tried a further variation. Since Amy had been engaging in her affair all this time without him knowing it, and life had been reasonably harmonious between them, though of course deeply dissatisfying for both, he would simply unknow what he had discovered, since he was not meant to know it in the first place.

Or was he? That was the only issue that spoke to him: the way his wife had used his daughter. Or the way Dana had decided to volunteer the information—for herself, by herself, and for him too. He had to consider that possibility. It was the most positive one in the field.

They marched through customs with their carry-on and their entry-level duty-free French wine. On the other side of the barrier, he and Amy embraced as Dana looked on, curious at the adult charade. He took in the new Amy, who was and was not new. He didn't remember seeing her in that dress before. He tried out the woeful practice of biased scanning. Were roses blooming on his wife's cheeks? Was her body fuller and shapelier and imprinted with the loving caresses of another hand?

"Let's go, I'm hungry," Dana piped up helpfully. "The food on the plane was crap."

It was her new sacred mission: giving her father a break by doing his share of the talking along with hers. She was prodigiously helpful on the way back to the house, and he made a note to thank her, and promise her this would not be a life-long role. That night, after the dinner Amy had cooked for the family and the emptying of the duty-free Bordeaux, he lay down next to her in the marriage bed. He felt her waiting. Has she defiled it, or wouldn't she dare with Megan lurking in the basement? *Defile*, he thought, *adultery*—such nineteenth-century terms in this modern life of theirs. Amy did not feel any different, though he didn't try anything. It would have been indecent and a cliché, trying to reclaim his territory, though he moved an inch closer to breathe in her perfume. It was no tangier, no muskier, no more alluring, no more complex. What was supposed to happen to a woman when she took a lover? Clearly, everything. Clearly, nothing. So it really wouldn't be such an accomplishment to unknow. His wife had had a reputedly life-changing experience, and he would ignore it. That didn't sound very feasible.

In the middle of the night he awoke with the sleep disarray of jetlag. It was the dead of night in the house of unsolvable things, but dawn in his brain. He had travelled enough to expect this sort of intrusion, and knew it was futile to fight it. He rose from the bed as his wife wrapped the sheet around her body to protect her rest. Sleep on, darling.

He stepped into the hallway and had a jetlag thought. What seemed at first like tattling or gossip was Dana sending him a message about something deeper. What it was, he did not know. Not yet. He closed the bedroom door. A house is a living being. It leans upon its inhabitants. It has its politics. That much he understood from what Jake Boeder had built for his parents.

Every room belonged to a family member. In this house, Dana had the lair of disorder in her room. Megan had her basement playhouse, though he would have never called it that to her face. Amy occupied the master bedroom that she had renamed the mistress bedroom. Where was his room? He had no room of his own. His occupation was fleeting. Currently, it was right here by the window that looked onto the street where autumn was beginning to show itself in the dry leaves that hung limply from their newly planted tree, still spindly and not assured of survival, that stood on the lawn in front of their house. Outside, a squad car moved soundlessly down the empty street. The car made no noise at all—were the police patrolling with electric vehicles now? The spot where he stood belonged to everyone and no one, certainly not to him exclusively. There was a desk in a wider space in the hall where he worked at night, at times like this. During the day he used a small table in the bedroom after Amy went to work. When she was late and hurried, she would leave a bottle of perfume or a vial of essential oil next to his computer. What is an essential oil, he once asked her. Are there oils that are unessential? She didn't bother answering. He was playing the contrarian, she had no time for word games first thing in the morning, and neither did she appreciate his attitude when it came to the world of skin care. Here was another contradiction that explained everything, and nothing. She complained about her body that was beyond love while applying perfume and smoothing oils and creams onto it.

When he was working in Moscow, his interpreter and fixer explained to him that the concept of personal space did not exist in her country. Being alone with oneself was a foreign idea, though in Russian one might say *his spot* for the place a person occupied. He did not like what his spot in this house said about him. He stretched out on the living room couch like a hapless husband. If he'd had boys, he would have gone into one of their rooms and lay down on their bed to spend the hours until morning came. But which boy would he have chosen? The question of favourites would not go away. Megan was right. Dana was his favourite. The missing piece, the troubled mind—what could be more attractive than that? The intrigue. The chance she might need him.

He got up a few minutes later, after something approximating sleep on the couch, and went to his desk in the hallway. Jetlag was handing him this opportunity, and he would be ungrateful to refuse it. His computer glowed happily when he turned it on. He was in a state of unreal suspension, a fugue state. He knew this sort of thing could happen. It was part of the dangers of the trade. He physically felt he was walking down the tractor path across the great Balkan plain outside Šid. He was in the school in Pančevo with its blown-out windows, where no one would ever learn anything again. He was in the crammed motel room that smelled of frightened men, where Dragan reached out and caressed the mattress on which a half-dozen refugees lay bunched together. It was to his advantage to be in those places, in that state of hyper-arousal, instead of here, in his house among the fields. That was the definition of traumatic attachments, and they had powered his work from the beginning. He believed he was someone else, somewhere else, in that way he was like most every other person on earth. He loved the sardonic, heartfelt masculine comedy he found on these trips, and he loved Dragan. He wondered how he might slip that moment in the motel into his story. As he worked on the piece and the light began to edge into the hallway from the living room windows, his super-ego and censor Susan returned to perch on his shoulder. He had swept off Anne Sheridan, only to have Susan alight in the doctor's place.

The bedroom door opened and Amy stepped out in the dressing gown he had bought her some years before. She squinted at him.

"I guess I don't need to ask what you're doing."

"I have a real nasty deadline. My editor is afraid she'll be scooped, or that some other crisis will come along and put this one out of business. I told her there was no chance of that happening, but she's nervous. I promised to finish ASAP."

His voice was thrumming with tight self-control. Amy went back into the bedroom, and a minute later he heard the shower running.

"Don't worry, we'll have plenty of time to talk."

But of course she couldn't hear him.

When she left the house for her job at the hospital, a well-paid ordeal since there was a new health care crisis every day, he moved to his desk in the bedroom. Over the years, he and his colleagues had devised a faithful trick of the trade. When they wrote a piece, they pictured the person they were writing for, someone they wanted to impress, a person whose love they strove for, which meant it was almost never their editor. They worked specifically for that one man or woman.

Phil didn't have that person yet. He figured he would find out who it was by writing the piece.

Dana never entered her parents' room, and neither did Megan. It was as rigid a rule as the one set down in Leviticus about not uncovering the nakedness of your father and mother, but unlike Leviticus, in this house it was unwritten. But the next day as Phil sat working on the refugee piece, he looked up and found Dana standing next to him. She glanced at the marriage bed. Its sheets were as stiffly tucked in and symmetrical as the ones in hospitals.

"Aren't you going to do anything about it?"

"Yes. When I finish this. Soon, trust me. In the meantime, I'm trying to think of some way that's original."

"Why does it have to be original? I mean, what do you *feel*?"

The question was fantastic. It came from a strange and ideal world where a daughter cared about her father's feelings, though the question was completely forbidden. If Leviticus were being written today, there would surely be an injunction against uncovering the nakedness of your parents' emotions.

"You said you looked up having an affair on the Internet. I'm sure you saw there are generally a lot of tears and screaming and recrimination and even tragedy. I'm going to try and not do that, if possible."

"Megan cries when she breaks up with her boyfriends. Even if she's the one who's breaking it up."

"How come you know that?"

"Come on, Dad, I can't tell you everything." She paused for effect. "Anyway," she told him airily, "as far as I'm concerned you don't have to do anything at all."

"Oh, no? I thought… "

"Really. I mean it. Listen to me. Now that the secret is out I feel freer. Weird, but true. I don't know why but that's the way it is."

"It might be interesting to know. But in the meantime, just be happy. Enjoy the windfall!"

"I'll think about it. Now I'll let you work. You need to finish."

He smiled at her. "You're a sneaky one. You know that when I finish, I'll have to *do something*."

Dana laughed. It was an acknowledgement.

"Do whatever you want. Do unconventional."

Then she turned and left, her message delivered. He watched her go, and wondered. If a person suddenly felt free, or freer, the basic human need to know why must kick in. Dana must have asked herself that question. Phil was stymied. A mother's secret affair is pushed out into the open, and her daughter feels better. She feels freer.

How does that work? He would need to start with what made her unhappy and unfree in the first place.

He put aside the Balkan refugees a moment.

Let's say she was forced to carry a secret, and then she freed herself of that debt to her mother by talking about it to the person least supposed to know. Too simple, Phil thought. Too melodramatic. Give me something more twisty. He turned to his fixer, driver, and amateur psychiatrist, Dragan. But not the real Dragan, the inner one he kept on hand. Dragan worked on the edges of a society on edge, he was no doctor of the mind, but he saw the world with the kind of stark knowledge Phil didn't have because of the conventions he carried. The inner Dragan was simply himself grown lucid, and no longer hoping to please. Phil beckoned, and out he popped from his chest like a jack-in-the-box with a glass of *rakija* in one hand and a bottle of mineral water in the other, and his sunglasses wedged between his fingers. He offered his patented ironic Balkan smile. It is simple, he told Phil. Your daughter has been liberated by her mother's affair. It is strange, but there is stranger. Look at it this way. She thought she would have to have a marriage like yours if she grew up, the whole sad unsolvable business, you will forgive me, but now she sees that doesn't have to be her fate. She has freedom to choose. That is good, but it creates one problem for you as a man. You now hold the proof that your wife really did have the affair, which you had to doubt at first, of course, the way we all would. But knowing you as I do, you will think it is a small price to pay for your daughter feeling better. What a strange path wellness takes! *Wellness*—that is the word? I heard it on a British television show. It doesn't sound like a real word, but who knows.

Then Dragan dematerialized like the Cheshire cat. He was only one of the things Phil brought back from this latest trip, and what a trophy he was. Though Dragan, of course, had been in him the whole while.

Phil took a breath and tried to think. Dana wanted the affair to come out into the open. No one made her into a messenger and sent her on a mission by remote control. It was terrible to have thought that, and have underestimated a girl as brilliant as she was, and as determined. She called down crisis on the house, which was why she was pushing him to *do something*. She wanted change. There had been times when she could not leave her room, but at this crucial moment she didn't back down from instability. She was going to air out the house. She was ready for whatever that might mean.

Phil pictured himself at her age. He wouldn't have had such daring. He paid no attention to adults, he couldn't have calculated what they might do under pressure. And he never considered refusing to grow up. The question did not occur to him as it had to Dana—as a choice she might make. Growing up must have changed, or it was different for girls, or for the girl Dana was. When he was a boy he wanted to get the hell out of Jake Boeder's house and go mix it up on his own and get hurt if that was the cost, he was more than willing to get hurt and the world only too happy to supply the pain. That was how he learned his job, and how he got good at it. He had no thought about choice. There was only flight forward, chaotic and reckless and with no consideration for whoever was in his path. Dana was a better person than he'd been at her age.

Either that, or simply female.

Phil Brenner turned in a record-breaking performance for the fastest completion of a think piece about the refugee trail through the Balkans. His feat earned him a second invitation to lunch from Susan. He owed his speedy, concentrated work to Amy.

"I'd love to meet you again," he told Susan over the phone. "I don't get downtown enough."

"Tell me again why you live out there in the fields… Oh, yes, that's what your wife wanted."

"I'm glad you remember. I hardly do."

"That's only because you're used to it!"

She snorted into the phone, then named the time and place. When it finally rolled around, lunch with Susan ended up being a hurried, fretful exercise, and a disappointment at first. A last-minute meeting kept her on edge and fiddling with her phone. He proposed a glass of wine to toast the completion of their project. She waved him off.

"This time it's my treat," he promised.

"Do you think I'll change my mind if you tell me you're paying?"

A second later she caught herself. "I'm sorry, it's been a rotten day."

"What's happening?"

To Phil's surprise, she confided in him. "Don't tell anyone, but the parent company wants to close us down. No, not close us down—send us into space. Cyberspace. We'll be nothing but digital by this time next year. You know, the ascendancy of the little screen and all that."

"You'll still have a job, won't you?"

She shook her head. "No. Yes. I suppose so. The big magazine on a little screen—I don't see it working, not with our design values."

He had considered Susan too harshly, as a woman who would be okay with any business model as long as she got paid to believe in it. He took her for a businesswoman who happened to alight in the world of magazines, but she turned out to have the same secret love of paper he did.

"I will have that glass of wine after all. Maybe it'll make me say something to those monkeys that I'll regret."

The service was snappy. No one had time to waste in this lunch spot. Phil raised his glass. "To regret. And to print."

"They do seem to be going hand in hand these days."

"And here I thought I was the only one in mourning for paper."

She gave him an appraising look that was not particularly friendly. "You always were that way. Convinced of your absolute originality. That makes it hard to see other people."

Then her device went off. Another surprise: her ring tone played "I Heard it through the Grapevine." It must have been authority calling. She did all the listening. At the end of the conversation she got to her feet.

"I have to go. Sorry to run out on you. Are you really paying?"

"A promise is a promise."

She picked up her glass, examined it a moment, then drank the wine that remained.

"Remember to say something you'll regret."

"I already have."

Then she went out the door. *Absolute originality*. The originality lay in her insult. He never thought she had it in her, which proved her point. He didn't see past his idea of her. A common fault, and nothing original at all.

Still, as he paid and left, he felt chastened. He had overlooked Susan the first time, and then now, decades later. Time was reputed to make people wiser, but it had not helped him much.

On the sidewalk, he got on the phone to Bruno.

"Got time to kill?"

"Kill time before it kills you."

"I'm downtown. I'll be there soon. I have a thirst for the eternal."

"Bad news," Bruno said mournfully. "I am abstaining."

"Don't worry, we can still be friends. We don't need drink."

"Don't make me laugh!"

A half-hour later, he found Bruno in his self-portrait of an apartment, staring balefully at a glass of water.

"You want to hear something?" Phil asked him.

"Should I plug my ears?"

"My wife had an affair. Is having an affair." He held up his hand to silence his friend. "And I have the craziest idea. I'm not going to do anything about it."

"You mean you won't kill her? Not even kill the guy?"

"Worse—I won't even discuss it. I won't engage."

Bruno shook his head. "She will hate you for that, you being so superior and all. You have conquered the heights of cruelty. You should be put in prison. But you get full credit for originality."

"You're the second person who's called me 'original' today. The first time it was an insult. This time too, I think. But that's what I'm trying to do. You know, defeat the convention."

"It sounds inhuman. Does she know you know?"

"She emailed me her confession. Sent me a scan."

"How tasteful. How modern. I can't blame you for wanting to strike back. But how long can you go on with this pretense and ignore her cry for help? And what will happen next?"

"I don't know."

Of all the things Phil expected Bruno to say, he did not expect this. His friend was right. He was practicing a cruel game, an attempt at vengeance disguised as serenity, as if he were a monk on a mountaintop. He did not know how to talk about what was going on, so he ignored it. That was a shopworn strategy, and certainly a normal first reaction. But he needed to move on to something else. He tried on this picture: sitting down with Amy at the Doll's House, because this kind of thing could not be discussed in the midst of domestic detail with the girls around. As Amy looked on, he grasped for a way to begin, but his lips would not form the words. After his initial stroke of originality, the ground fell away beneath him. The serenity strategy was designed to protect him from that feeling. Now it was gone. He would have to go to Amy and try something.

"I don't know what to do," he told Bruno.

"First, avoid alcohol and sharp objects. And consider that jealousy is involved with the fear of annihilation, which is greater than the ordinary fear of death. 'There was someone before me. There will be someone after me. I will cease to exist.' It is the great mandala, or whatever you call it. Something circular that makes us disappear."

Bruno stood up and went into the kitchen.

"Great news," he called from the sink. "I found the corkscrew since your last visit."

"I thought you were abstaining."

"I am. But for certain solemn occasions, we must break our resolve. You would do the same for me."

"I would never have made that resolution in the first place."

"That's because you're moderate."

Phil didn't feel very moderate. If you feel bad, don't do anything that will make you feel worse—a sad joke.

Bruno was a fan of the big-shouldered wines from Spain, the ones you had to chew before you swallowed. The glass drunk quickly in the restaurant with Susan had been calling out for a companion, and finally here it was.

Bruno let the mouth of the bottle hover over his glass.

"I won't pour until you promise me you will not go home afterward and start talking to your wife about this business. You will not be in proper shape."

Phil promised. "Avoid alcohol and annihilation."

"You learn fast."

Bruno was quiet and gentle with Phil's loss. He gave him no further advice, and did not dip into his vast treasure house of stories of female betrayal that had wounded him even without the institution of marriage to legitimize the hurt. That was the gift of friendship: mere presence was a balm. Drinking in the afternoon was new to Phil, and it posed a particular set of challenges. He could not fall into bed and proclaim the evening ended. He had to be somewhere and someone later on, a father if called upon, a reasonable facsimile of a husband. Where was Amy right now, he wondered, and he reached for his phone to call her. Then he checked his resolve. It was just the kind of alcoholic decision-making he had promised to avoid. She wouldn't have answered. She was probably engaging in afternoon delight, the best hours for love. He had not known daylight on naked skin for years.

"You are feeling sorry for yourself," Bruno told him. "Also best avoided. The way you should avoid getting into bed with the grief counselling woman."

"The therapist?"

"No, the one you consoled."

"Lynne." Phil said her name. It echoed with sudden power, and he listened to it. "But I want to."

"Of course. At least that means you are still alive, and have some shreds of self-confidence left."

Dr. Sheridan had given him the same advice, though Bruno and she were at opposite ends of any imaginable moral spectrum. *A bed of loss.* What Dragan called *unsolvable.* Anne Sheridan was of no further use to Phil. If he exposed his situation with his wife to her, she would cheer Amy on like a pom-pom girl. He was without a therapist, on his own. He would have to be his own therapist. He tried on that new position, and a possibility jumped out. What if Amy's affair was her response to loss? If that was true, he should be more compassionate and less scheming. A woman who claimed she had no loss was vulnerable to any number of strategies.

He had come to Bruno's house expecting cynical and possibly vengeful advice, and his friend spared him. A good thing. That talk would have wounded his already unsteady heart. Dana, Susan, and now Bruno. People were surprising him. That was a positive sign. He still had the capacity to be surprised. His friends were true friends, not just people he thought he knew everything about, cases with behaviors he could anticipate, agreeable or irritating, depending on the mood. The atmosphere in Bruno's apartment was mild, soft and almost lyrical, and that mood deepened as the afternoon passed. He asked his friend if he could nap on the couch with its crosshatch of Abyssinian cat hairs.

"You can move in," Bruno told Phil, "if you are looking for an alternative to the conventional."

Then the time came when Phil and Amy could not ignore the situation anymore. They were, after all, still technically married. Their children forced the opportunity on them. Dana had been going out one night out of two, destination unknown, since she returned from the trip, and Megan came all the way upstairs to announce she was going to a pho restaurant with Tyler and his parents. How obviously the girls telegraphed their intentions, and how moving they were, setting the tender trap for their messed-up parents.

Once they filed out, Phil called to his wife from a further room.

"I'm going to get the car washed!"

"I can't hear you!"

He went into the kitchen to tell her again, and that was his fatal misstep. Amy had set a bottle of white wine and a tray of olives on the table. Phil evaluated the props of the romantic encounter. They stood for something else now—the guillotine.

"Do we really have to?"

"You deserve a medal for avoidance. How long have you been back?"

"I've been busy."

"And you can do only one thing at a time."

"Exactly. And I did it. Do you want my blessing? In divorce proceedings, that used to be called collusion. But I don't want a divorce."

Amy veered off into safer, common territory. "Your trip changed Dana. I thought it was a terrible idea at first. It seems I was wrong."

"We had to do something to break her out of that room. Though she wasn't really in there all the time, as I finally realized."

"We were both in there with her."

"She is the most important relationship in my life—with Megan too, of course. Both of them. That is where I can still do some good. That's where it would hurt most if I failed."

Amy listened to her husband's words. They were harsh, but they did make sense. Why would a man, a husband, linger over the woman who had stopped bringing him pleasure? Phil had not planned to say what he said, though he did understand lately that what he wanted most at this point in his life was to have the feeling of doing some good for someone. After the trip with Dana and the things she told him, he felt elated. It was a feeling close to happiness, a true emotional accomplishment. He didn't think that was possible at this age, and even less so thanks to a daughter who had spent half her life being a problem child.

"You'll be happy to know I've stopped seeing the therapist. Dr. Sheridan."

"Because of Dana?"

"No. I didn't like certain things she said about men. They were gender stereotypes."

Amy smiled, and he did not like her smile. No doubt she held the same views as Anne Sheridan. "She let you stop?"

"I'm bigger and meaner than her. I walked out the door."

"So now you are free of loss."

"No. No one is free of loss, and you know that. That's what we're talking about. Anyway," he added, "we agreed at the start that we weren't going to discuss my adventures in therapy."

"You brought up the subject."

He had, but only as a diversion.

They sat across from each other at their kitchen table. The reputed gladdening effects of wine ran off his heart and did not penetrate it. On this occasion he was stronger than alcohol, tenser, and he regretted his strength. He wanted to surrender to the seduction scene, but what would he be surrendering to?

"My problem is that I can't find a good way to talk about what's happening with you," he told his wife. "I suppose that's a blessing, at least for now. If I do come up with a way, I'll let you know right away."

Then he stood, took his glass and drank it off.

"You're looking good these days." She brushed off the compliment the way she always did. "Now, I really am going to get the car washed."

His daughters would be disappointed. They had set the tender trap, and no reconciliation scene had occurred. At least there wasn't a cooked rabbit waiting in a pot on the stove. He simply could not have the conversation indicated for such a common event as this. She had set out the olives and the wine, but beyond that, Amy was of absolutely no help.

As he sat parked in the line in front of the no-touch car wash with his coupon in hand that was set to expire today, his phone began sending him distress messages. He could not read the call display without his reading glasses, and he had left them at the house due to his quick exit. The only way to find out who it was would be to answer. If it's Amy… No, that wouldn't be like her. It's Susan. She's gotten the sack, she wants to discuss employment opportunities.

"Is everything all right with you?"

It was Lynne.

"I'm waiting at the car wash. Why?"

"Dr. Sheridan had another reception and you didn't show. It's not like you to boycott and miss all the fun. I figured something must be up."

"She didn't invite me, that's what's up. I've been cast out of the inner circle. Here I was, trying to be so likeable, and I get excluded."

"You must have done something that deserved punishment," Lynne countered.

"I suppose I did. Look, I've got to go, it's my turn to get washed."

Just as he was entering the tunnel of rain, she invited him to drop by, or at least that was what he understood. Access was suddenly permitted, and he hadn't requested it. The waves of water and the magic caress of no-touch brushes obliterated the signal.

As the artificial monsoon washed over him, he wondered what would happen if he opened the car door and stepped out into the storm. Had anyone done that? Someone must have, some poor man who very badly wanted to come clean, and be cleansed by a bone-breaking assault of high-pressure hoses and industrial solvents. Someone really desperate. That wouldn't be him. He had done nothing wrong. If anything, he was pure to a fault.

On the far side of that speculation, he dialed Lynne's number as the water dripped off the car.

"Thanks for calling back. I know girls aren't supposed to call boys, but after you didn't come to her soirée, I started wondering why."

"Well, now you know. And I was overseas for work. But I've been thinking of you. I have a lot to tell you."

"Not about loss, I hope."

"No. About found."

"That sounds positive for once."

"Rare, for sure. I'd be glad to see your unit again."

"What the hell are you talking about?"

"Your condo. That's what you called it once: your unit."

She insisted she had never said any such thing.

Phil went to the liquor store on the way to Lynne's place. He looked at the line of refrigerated whites. He couldn't remember if she favoured white over red, or if it mattered. Then he remembered the smudge of red on her mouth the evening he met her, the two glasses in her hand, and her surprise assertion that she was his loss. But she was wrong. Their spirited beginning did have some continuity. He might not have found her, but neither had he lost her entirely.

He chose a bottle of something called "Le Vin Noir," black wine. A wine by that name promised smudges.

At the door to her place he presented Lynne with his gift, and she seemed happy enough with the choice. Once she uncorked it, and they settled onto the cream-coloured sofa, Phil launched into his good news. She listened. She was puzzled. It was not often that a married man considered being cuckolded a source of enthusiasm and joy. What kind of man would think that way? My kind, Phil assured her. Forgive me if I am incredulous, she told him.

Then she tried to put the strange event into her own words. A woman's words. Here was his daughter Dana, feeling freer, feeling better, talking frankly and inquiringly and even empathetically because her mother was having an affair, out in the open. *Because*—no doubt it was not so simple as cause-and-effect. The girl, Lynne speculated, was taking on her mother's sexuality, and the presumed liberation that follows when a wife steps outside the bonds of a tired marriage.

"Though usually a daughter pushes away her mother's sexuality," Phil countered.

"So they say." Lynne was unimpressed. "But your daughter isn't much for conventional morality. That's to your credit. Or hers."

"Yes. She could have disowned her mother, or gotten high-and-mighty about that thing called 'cheating.' The only negative thing she had to say was that her mother was too old to have an affair."

Lynne laughed, and Phil joined her happily. In their glasses, the black wine was opaque, like water in a cypress swamp.

"No one can tell whether she won't arrive at that point later on."

"The way my daughter disowned me."

They sat in that sombre atmosphere a moment.

"But that might change. I mean, your daughter's attitude. Isn't that the purpose of the program she's in?"

"The stated purpose, yes. Rebuilding self-esteem. But it's more like a re-education camp that teaches kids to hate their families."

"That's just a step. You know, like homeopathy. You have to get sick and hate before you can get better and love."

"Aren't you in an optimistic mood. Did they change your medication?"

Lynne lifted her glass and took a deep drink of wine. It made a wonderful smudge on her lips. He would tell her that later, maybe. It could wait.

"That's something we share, Lynne. Our primary relationships are with our daughters."

"Primary relationships. You make it sound like polyamory with a rating system of points for the partner you most prefer." She stood up. "Here. You stand up too."

He did as she told.

"You can hold me now. It'll make up for the last time when I didn't want to. Don't be afraid."

He did the wise thing. He didn't say he wasn't afraid. Because he was. He didn't particularly want to embrace the scarecrow woman again.

"All the time I was watching Dana's new way of being, and listening to her talk, those amazing things she was saying, I thought of you. I wanted something like that for you."

"There's absolutely no comparison. But you cared, and that's nice."

He stepped away from her.

"When people get better, where does their illness go? It can't just disappear, and be lost. It must go someplace."

Lynne laughed unhappily. "To the nightmare zone, probably. Where it waits for the next victim."

"If I could go there, I would. I would bring back reconciliation for the two of you."

"You'd go into the underworld for me?"

"I would. And stay as long as necessary."

She pressed her body against him. She was trembling. He didn't think this could possibly turn out well. Then he understood she was crying.

There were plenty of good reasons to cry. Maybe she had invited him over so she could cry. She pulled away and looked at him.

"I guess I should ask what you're going to do about it. Your wife's affair, I mean."

With the tears on her face and her red eyes, it looked like he had just confessed to betraying her.

"Nothing," he said.

"Nothing?"

"Yes. I've been called cruel and unusual by my best friend for that."

"She must be disappointed. Your wife, I mean. She went to all that effort. And then, nothing. No reaction."

"I would do something if I could," he said stiffly.

"It must be strange. I mean, here you are, faced with this supposedly dramatic, life-changing, marriage-ending event, and then... you do nothing."

"It can't be that life-changing if everyone is doing it."

"I didn't do it when I was married."

"That must happen more often than people think. We have a big experience, but we end up on the outside of it."

"Let me be your therapist for thirty seconds. You can pay what you want." She counted out the possibilities on her fingers. "Denial of pain. Betrayal. Alienation. Dissociation."

"None of that sounds very good."

"Maybe it's a case of loss."

"Everything is."

"But this definitely is."

"Okay, you're right. Only I don't exactly know what I've lost."

"I don't believe you," she told him. "Start with trust, maybe."

Then Lynne shrugged off her own words. She had no interest in being right. He looked past her, around the room. There were startling new additions since the last time. A picture on the wall, the portrait of a house with a long curving entryway like a tongue leading to a mouth. It must take forever to reach the front door. That could have been the point. And then, a piece of Maghreb textile in clay-coloured tones. She was working on her interior. It was getting dangerously close to warm in here.

"It's beginning to look like someone actually lives here."

"Yes. I'm sorry. I don't know what came over me."

He looked past this slightly warmer room into Lynne's bedroom. She had undertaken no decorating work there. From where he stood, the setting where intimacy was meant to occur had all the appeal of a hospital chamber. The blank walls, the sheets tucked tightly over the mattress, the violent creases of the bedspread, not a single concession to beauty, even a mirror. But that did not matter. He and Lynne had done everything possible to make sure they would not end up in there.

Still, he imagined doing the impossible, which he had done many times when he was younger. Taking her hand, telling her she was beautiful to him, listening to his inner Bruno who whispered to him that Lynne had called after an evening when she had expected to see him and did not, doesn't that mean anything to you, you have done enough consoling, maybe it is time to love her.

But Phil did none of those things. When he imagined holding Lynne close, her daughter, still unnamed, slipped into the narrow interstice between them, an unquiet, unavenged spirit. He felt her wounded body in Lynne's, and did not want to repeat the abuse, the way Lynne went passive, and would not lift her arms from her sides, even as he allowed him to hold her this time, like a dare or a favour returned.

Lynne's daughter was not alone. Dana was watching him too, unblinking. If you don't want to do conventional, the way you say you don't, then don't do this.

Some weeks later, Lynne had news for him. Good or bad? he asked. You decide, she said. He was about to offer to come to her place but everything tumbled out at once, over the phone. Her husband—sorry, her ex-husband—had gotten sloppy with his colleagues at the college pub one evening not long ago and blurted out this incredible piece of pop wisdom: most people have their first sexual experience in the home. In the wider sense, Godbold was right. The glimpse of the parents together in the bedroom, a sister stepping out of the shower as her towel gapes open, a big brother caught masturbating. But Godbold did not give any such examples of those common moments his colleagues might have shared. And he made his declaration in front of exactly the wrong person, a fellow teacher and local talent on the academic poetry scene whose daughter had been interfered with by his wife's brother. The man's name was McGraff, and he immediately got a bad feeling about Godbold. The feeling became a certainty through the evening as he listened to Godbold. He even stopped drinking to make sure his senses stayed sharp. And they did. It was the man's complete sense of entitlement—that was McGraff's tipoff. The next week when he knew his colleague was busy at the college, he went to Godbold's house and knocked on the door in the afternoon after grade school had let out. He quizzed his wife on the subject. McGraff had deep knowledge of the issue that was born of misfortune, and he asked the right questions. Had the second Godbold girl, whose name was Jackie, begun acting provocatively for her age? Had she started using unusual sexual vocabulary or odd key words? Was she touching herself in inappropriate places and at inappropriate times?

The girl was a textbook case. She displayed all those symptoms. For what seemed like a lifetime, she had been grasping for a way to say what was happening to her. Now, thanks to a stranger who knew everything about her, that way opened up. Jackie had slipped into the living room of the family house and heard everything McGraff said. She stood behind her mother who had not noticed her because she was busy talking to the man who had come out of nowhere to save her daughter, and Jackie did more than tell. She tore up the family contract into a thousand noisy pieces.

"We'll see if that helps my daughter," Lynne told Phil.

"It can't be a bad thing. Will he be charged for her too?"

"We're well within the statute of limitations. Trust me, I know them by heart. But I'm not sure what'll happen. If my daughter defends him this time, I'll die."

"In the end, a perfect stranger helped you. This McGraff."

"Which makes sense. Everyone else who knew protected him. It's the nature of the family."

"I was waiting for you to say that."

"You still don't believe me?"

"I do. I always have."

That wasn't the whole truth, but it became the truth now.

He put down the phone. This will change Lynne's life, he thought. Though the loss will remain.

On the afternoon of the failed tender trap, Phil had rushed off to the carwash, and the unexpected rendezvous that followed, and what he had hoped to say about Dana to his wife remained unspoken. His refugee piece had come out, rushed into publication without grievous errors. It was first praised and soon forgotten, though it did return later on the shortlist of the year's best magazine stories.

In the meantime, he and Amy coexisted as a long-term balancing act. He continued to live in unknowing of much of what happened under his roof. Essential things, though not knowing them did not change his life, so how essential were they?

And then, one evening, months later, the unknowing ended. He was standing next to Amy in the living room as she sat in front of the screen. She hit the remote, and Netflix came on with its usual offers. He hovered for a moment to see what she would choose. The usual fare was tough-minded lady detectives from the northern countries. They got things done, then went home to an empty house and drank a neat scotch or two. Occasionally they had a dead-end affair with a colleague. But best of all, they had the gift of making her husband disappear.

She put on her Netflix face, which was the fruit of exhaustion. Between announcing budget cuts and fielding hostile queries about *C. difficile*, it had been another lousy day. She more than earned her pay.

Amy looked up at him, as if surprised he was still there. She hit the remote again, and the screen went dark. Phil was alarmed. His escape was cut off.

"You should know, I ended the affair," she said.

"Just now?"

She waved the hand with the remote, a gesture toward a vague past.

"No. A while ago. After you and Dana came back."

"Your gentleman must have been surprised."

"Not at all. He always said the end was written into every affair a man might have with a married woman."

Amy stared at the unlit screen as if her story was being played out there, and she a character in this drama against convention. The blank slate of a dark screen seemed to inspire her.

"But it turned out that that was just a piece of male wisdom. He got emotional. He said I had a gift and he would miss it. He'd been the luckiest man in the world, and now he wasn't lucky anymore."

She cannot do this without taking her pound of flesh, Phil understood. It took all his discipline not to walk out of the room. He had been all right with unknowing.

"Well, you called him your primary relationship. If you've forgotten, I kept the document."

"Yes. I must have it as well." Amy looked up at Phil. "He told me I was precious to him. I've never heard a man say that word."

"You didn't tell me you started an affair," he said to his wife. "You could have not told me you ended it."

"I thought about that. I could have cultivated my secret, even if it held nothing. No, that's not true—it would still have had its potential, with all the things I experienced. I waited long enough. Anyway, how could I have told you? We weren't speaking to each other. And I didn't want you to think I was ending it for you, to get you back."

Amy had a gift for the unconventional. It made no sense to end the affair. She had some form of his blessing, call it complicity or collusion or freedom. And she'd never told her lover about Phil's lack of reaction, which she still insisted was a game he was playing, and not the mute expression of his dismay. But something strange happened. His lack of reaction had made her ashamed; it reflected badly on her.

"Besides," she continued, "I figured he would shy away from me if I suddenly turned out to be free, freer than he was. The equation behind an affair is that neither party is ever truly available."

That was Amy through and through. She strategized for a living. Her way of being in the world. Phil kept those reflections to himself. This was a time to avoid anything that might sound like blame.

"And since I'm telling you things I shouldn't, though God knows why, I'll tell you one more. I understood it after the fact. I sent you my confession as a way of ending it. It could thrive and provide me pleasure only if it was secret."

"You ended it," he stated, "but it will never truly end."

"No. It will live on in your refusal to engage with me."

The Netflix menu came on again. He had only seconds left.

"I owe it all to you," he told Amy. "Everything good that's happened with Dana."

"Can I know what you're talking about?"

"You told her about your affair, and somehow that helped. She came out of herself. The trip was part of it, but mostly it was you. She changed for the better. She stopped being afraid of becoming a woman. I don't know why it worked that way, but it did."

"Why don't you ask your grief counsellor? But wait, you don't have her anymore. Or have you gone back?"

"Are you telling me you haven't noticed how Dana has changed?"

"I have. It was your trip. She told me about some things she saw. It affected her, obviously. At least I found out something about your adventures together. I mean, outside of reading your story where she doesn't appear."

"She was not the subject. But believe me, she is in every line."

"Maybe seeing all those things made her bored with the way she was. That can happen. People get bored with themselves and change. It has nothing to do with me. That's absurd."

"Not to me."

"You can think whatever you like. But please don't impose your opinions on Dana."

He wasn't imposing anything on his daughter. The idea had come from her.

"You can stop living for Dana, now that you're satisfied with how she's doing."

"I have," he told Amy.

"Good. I lived for my children long enough."

"And then you did something for yourself."

"And then I undid it." She turned her eyes away from Phil. She was afraid of the next emotion.

If children need to free themselves from their parents, Phil thought, the opposite must be true too. Amy's affair was part of that self-freeing. He found no satisfaction in what she had told him tonight. He still could not think past the journal pages slowly scrolling open on his computer screen. That was a shame. For a woman who had enjoyed new love, and then chosen to end it, both acts of power, she did not look very happy. His friend Bruno was right. He had hurt her by not engaging with her. He was overly proud of refusing conventions. Maybe he had turned inhuman in the process. She hadn't wanted to spend the rest of her life sleeping with the same man. There was nothing unusual about that. There was nothing more human, as opposed to his unhuman reaction. If only she had managed it differently, and not involved Dana, not sent her scanned confession when he was in a precarious spot, they would not be at this point. If only she had offered a word or two of understanding, a way of helping him assimilate what she had done.

The menu on the screen asked Amy to make her choice. Their conversation wasn't over. Phil did not know exactly what that meant. He didn't want the convention of the reconciliation scene, though he did understand that life without any conventions is a form of unlivable extremism, emotional terrorism for everyone involved. Perhaps he would make peace with the imperfections of his life. From what he understood from the people around him, this was a common enough adult practice, even something of an art form. It was not a life of union, but maybe it was not as inglorious as he had always considered.

In his younger life he had the moral ambition of being a person who does good for others. A laudable striving, but he never got anywhere near to fulfilling it. He had been that person with Dana. He had tried with Lynne, and recognized their limits, which in itself was a moral act. As he left the room and with it the Netflix stories of female efficiency and solitude, he resolved not to let Lynne drift away from him and allow herself to be forgotten. Because when a person tells you that she is your loss, it's because she wants to be found.

He had no clear idea what that would mean for him. But he was out of the slump, and he sensed it was for good.

ESPLANADE
Books

THE FICTION IMPRINT AT VÉHICULE PRESS

A House by the Sea : A novel by Sikeena Karmali
A Short Journey by Car : Stories by Liam Durcan
Seventeen Tomatoes : Tales from Kashmir : Stories by Jaspreet Singh
Garbage Head : A novel by Christopher Willard
The Rent Collector : A novel by B. Glen Rotchin
Dead Man's Float : A novel by Nicholas Maes
Optique : Stories by Clayton Bailey
Out of Cleveland : Stories by Lolette Kuby
Pardon Our Monsters : Stories by Andrew Hood
Chef : A novel by Jaspreet Singh
Orfeo : A novel by Hans-Jürgen Greif
[Translated from the French by Fred A. Reed]
Anna's Shadow : A novel by David Manicom
Sundre : A novel by Christopher Willard
Animals : A novel by Don LePan
Writing Personals : A novel by Lolette Kuby
Niko : A novel by Dimitri Nasrallah
Stopping for Strangers : Stories by Daniel Griffin
The Love Monster: A novel by Missy Marston
A Message for the Emperor : A novel by Mark Frutkin
New Tab : A novel by Guillaume Morissette
Swing in the House : Stories by Anita Anand
Breathing Lessons : A novel by Andy Sinclair
Ex-Yu : Stories by Josip Novakovich

The Goddess of Fireflies : A novel by Geneviève Pettersen
[Translated from the French by Neil Smith]
All That Sang : A novella by Lydia Perović
Hungary-Hollywood Express : A novel by Éric Plamondon
[Translated from the French by Dimitri Nasrallah]
English is Not a Magic Language : A novel by Jacques Poulin
[Translated from the French by Sheila Fischman]
Tumbleweed : Stories by Josip Novakovich
A Three-Tiered Pastel Dream : Stories by Lesley Trites
Sun of a Distant Land : A novel by David Bouchet
[Translated from the French by Claire Holden Rothman]
The Original Face : A novel by Guillaume Morissette
The Bleeds : A novel by Dimitri Nasrallah
Nirliit : A novel by Juliana Léveillé-Trudel
[Translated from the French by Anita Anand]
The Deserters : A novel by Pamela Mulloy
Mayonnaise : A novel by Éric Plamondon
[Translated from the French by Dimitri Nasrallah]
The Teardown : A novel by David Homel
Aphelia : A novel by Mikella Nicol
[Translated from the French by Lesley Trites]